I0543847

Woodland Fae

The World of Fae

Book 10

TERRY SPEAR

PUBLISHED BY:

Terry Spear

Woodland Fae

Copyright © 2018 by Terry Spear

Discover more about Terry Spear at:

http://www.terryspear.com/

ISBN-13: 978-1-63311-042-7

DEDICATION

Thanks so much to Sarah Quiring for being excited to read the newest edition of The World of Fae! We all need a little fantasy in our lives, right?

ACKNOWLEDGMENTS

Thanks so much to Donna Fournier and Darla Taylor for helping me to get this ready for all my readers! It's nearly Christmas and I couldn't be more excited to share it with everyone, and thanking the ladies once again!

CHAPTER 1

"Where's Bryan?" dragon fae shifter Ena asked, as she and her mate, Brett, and others of her household sat down to eat the morning meal at her castle. Well, it was now *Brett's* and *her* castle. She wasn't quite used to thinking of it in that way. Dragons didn't share. What was theirs was theirs. So this was a totally new experience for her.

She swore Brett's human friend Bryan ate more than anyone else in their household, though she had to admit the human and his friend Mark had worked wonders on her gardens. So much so that her dragon shifter friend Alton, who was known to have beautiful gardens, tried to steal Bryan and Mark away from her with a bribe of treasure untold.

Alton should have known it wouldn't work. Not when her mate, Brett, mage, phantom fae, and dragon shifter, was a good friend of both the teens when they'd lived in the human world. Friendship trumped treasure in their book. Besides, Ena paid them plenty of her own treasure to keep them satisfied and working hard.

Lila, her cook, served more eggs and cinnamon rolls, the sweet confections were some of Brett's favorites. Before Ena received Brett in payment for saving Princess Alicia, crown princess of the dragon fae, Brett had been a fae killer, but only of the unseelie kind. To his credit.

Everyone looked at Mark to see if he knew where Bryan was. The other human who'd joined the staff was also a fae seer like Bryan. If they were anything like Brett, they still might be fae, but just hadn't come into their fae powers yet. The problem was, what kind of fae would they be? Dragon fae didn't get along with all fae kinds.

Mark shrugged. "I wanted to start work on a water garden this morning—"

"Water garden?" Ena couldn't be more thrilled. She had told them she wanted them to plan the gardens, hoping they wouldn't make a mess of them. But she'd been thoroughly pleased to see the way the gardens were turning out.

She'd heard rumors that Queen Viviana, ruler of the dragon fae, would make Bryan and Mark *her* master gardeners at her castle, if she learned what miracles they had done with Ena's flowers, arbors, gazebos, and bridges, all making for the perfect getaway for Ena and Brett. After a harrowing, long day, or several, of taking

on missions—which was their dragon shifter heritage—
they needed the time to chill.

"Beg your pardon," Muriel, her lady's maid said,
"but Hannah left the castle. We're not sure when. Maybe
Bryan went with her? To look after her?"

To keep her in line? Ena frowned. Despite that the
human was a fae seer, who had used Bryan in an attempt
to lure the fae into a killing trap, and the leader of the
gang of thugs, Ena had allowed Hannah to live among
them—just in case she was truly a fae who had been
living with the humans. Her abilities just might not have
shown up yet. Mark and Bryan might be the same way,
which was part of the reason why they'd wanted to give
up killing the fae who dropped into the human world and
instead, seek out adventure in the fae world.

Both hoped they'd end up being like Brett, in his
words, a paladin, a great warrior, who was also a mage.
Though he said that the paladins he'd played in video
games weren't also dragon shifters. In truth, he'd turned
out to be a prince. Who would ever have thought that?
And *her* prince. Which meant, Ena was now a princess.
But she still was Ena, wearing her black corsets, form-
fitting leather pants, and boots and her black hair cut
short—her look, her way. On occasion, she did wear a
gown, just because she wanted to.

Bryan had been protective of Hannah, when no one
even liked the fae seer. She was belligerent, rude to
everyone, and even Ena's threat to turn her to toast—
using her dragon fire—had no effect. Hannah could have

at least pretended to be afraid of her. Ena even threatened to return her to her own world, let her face the consequences, should she be a true fae, show off her fae aura, and have to deal with the fae seers back home. They would want her blood.

"She'd better be working in the gardens." Ena knew the girl wasn't, but she wanted to impress upon Mark and Bryan that if Hannah slept in her castle and was given food and clothes, she had to work for the privilege. Ena had gotten way too lax with the human. She didn't want her other staff to feel they worked hard when some human didn't.

"She does," Mark said.

"Good, because I have half a mind to send her back to your people, the next time I hear she's caused anyone any trouble."

Mark looked at Brett, as if thinking he'd protect Hannah.

Brett shook his head. "Don't look at me. You and Bryan and I wanted to be here. Ena could be doing her a great service if Hannah turns out to be like me. Ena's right about Hannah working here and getting along. There's no reason to keep her here, if she continues to be so hateful."

Ena appreciated Brett's words of support, though she wouldn't have expected anything less from him. Her sparing his life had made him grateful to her beyond words. Not like Hannah.

"Do you want me to check Bryan's chamber and see

if he's sick?" Mark asked, sounding worried that Bryan could be running around somewhere with Hannah and getting himself into trouble.

"No, finish your breakfast. I can hardly wait to see what you come up with in the water garden, Mark." Ena knew he'd check on Bryan as soon as the meal was done. He may never be more than a human, but he and Bryan had grown on her. In part, because they'd helped her to fight her battles, but now also with creating beautiful gardens. She'd never dreamed hers would rival Alton's.

Every time Alton came over to see them, she swore his dragon shifter-golden fae mate Kayla, would console him that their gardens filled with lavender—her special gift—couldn't be beat. It was true that they received tons of income off her lavender, that was made into everything from seasonings and teas, to cloth dyes. Not only that, but Kayla had started a business of offering mushrooms on the side, but she wouldn't say where she was harvesting them from so she wouldn't have any competition.

Ena didn't blame her in the least. Fae could be untrustworthy.

After breakfast, Mark hurried off to see Bryan, as she knew he would. She and Brett had a mission to go on: look for a highly prized and well-loved goat this morning. They took their business of searching for lost objects and people seriously.

Brett wrapped Ena in his arms and kissed her. "Cook made those cinnamon rolls for you too, you know."

Ena arched a brow.

Brett smiled and kissed her mouth. "It didn't go unnoticed that you always eat two of them when she serves them. Lila was most pleased."

Ena hmphed. "She made them for you, because she knows how much that pleases *you*."

He smiled. "By making what I like, she discovered what you also like, since you'd never had them before." Then he frowned and ran his hand over her belly. "I know that you get a lot of exercise, but you seem to be gaining a bit of weight lately."

She glanced around the empty dining hall before she spoke softly to Brett. "I want to see the healer first to confirm this, but we *might* be having the first dragon shifter baby born here in years."

Brett smiled, looking pleased and she was glad.

"But, I don't want you to tell anyone yet, before it's a sure thing."

"I couldn't be happier, and before Alton and Kayla have any too."

She scoffed. "This is not a race." Though she knew Brett and Alton were always trying to outdo each other.

Mark rushed into the dining room, startling them and Ena knew right away he had bad news. "It's Bryan. He's in his bed, burning up with a fever and his skin is white as ice."

Muriel hurried into the dining room to join them. "I'll get the healer."

Ena hadn't expected that news. This was some of the

trouble they had with keeping humans in the fae world. They didn't heal as quickly as the fae did. And not as well on their own sometimes, depending on what ailed them.

"Some human illness?" Ena asked, and she and Brett hurried after Mark to see Bryan in his chamber.

"He won't say, but he looks like he's dying," Mark said, tears clogging his throat.

***

Gray wolf shifter Myla guarded the cave full of treasure for Alton and his mate Kayla, now, the wolves loving to do it because they could receive gold coins to pay for supplies. Many worked tree farms and other kinds of gardens, loving nature. She'd checked all the piles of treasure, smelled them, and knew her brother Simon had been here earlier. She'd relieved Clarita, a winged wolf shifter fae, but Myla's wolf family didn't have the wings. She thought they were cool and sometimes wished she had some too.

Nothing extraordinary had happened here in months, so she wasn't expecting any thieves to show up. Still, she always wore her wolf coat when she guarded the treasure, just in case.

She was glad she was in here, truth be told, because she had smelled the rains coming and liked a nice dry spot to stay in. Though their double coat of fur would keep the rain collecting on her outer guard hairs from reaching her skin.

She paced some more, then settled on the floor deep

inside the cave to wait for her shift to be over. It was an easy job and paid well. She never slept while she was here, but if she had fallen asleep, any little sound would have alerted her that something had moved inside the cave. Usually, it was just a mouse or a rat.

She needed something easy to do for the next four hours. She'd helped with her sister's rambunctious wolf pups for a couple of hours earlier, and though she adored them, the four were a handful.

And then she heard something that made her hackles raise. A wolf running into the cave. No one should be here, but then she suspected someone needed to tell her some news.

When the wolf finally made its appearance at the opening to the treasure room, Myla saw that she was a brown she-wolf, no one she'd ever seen before. She instantly jumped to her feet and growled low, warning the wolf to leave the cave at once. No wolves were allowed in here unless it was official pack business, or one of the wolves paid to guard the treasure.

When the wolf bared her teeth at Myla, she rushed forth to nip at her, to give her the message she couldn't be in here.

What Myla hadn't expected was for the wolf to come out of the dark and attack her! The creature didn't have any reason to come at her like that, unless she intended to steal some of Alton's treasure. She couldn't allow it and needed to alert the pack. Even though it was her job to protect it, the standing rule was to call for backup too, in the event of trouble.

Before she could howl to her pack, the wolf tore into her.

Myla knew the wolf was so vicious, she would kill her if she let down her guard. She fought with all the training she'd had over the years, play fighting with her brothers and sister and others in the Wolf Mountain pack. She'd never fought another wolf for real though.

She smelled her blood and she swore the attacking female was driven by the smell of blood. *Her* blood!

Myla was so busy fighting back, she didn't even feel the pain of her wounds. She growled and snarled as much as the attacking wolf did and got in a couple of bites that made the wolf dodge away from her. But she couldn't howl for help. Every time she tried to lift her chin to howl, the wolf raced forward and the two clashed again, snapping jaws, teeth scraping against teeth, except now Myla smelled the wolf's blood too.

Again, she tore into the wolf, tearing her ear flap and the aggressor ran off a little way, as if needing time to catch her breath before she charged in again.

Then they heard something—the sound of rain pouring down outside. And then something else. Someone coming, footfalls, a fae's, not a wolf's.

Before Myla could call out a warning to the newcomer, hoping it wasn't this wolf's accomplice, the brown wolf swung around and attacked her again.

***

Letta had finally left King Tameron and her people

behind in the woodland community where they lived to start out on her own, like any of the scorpion fae had to do when he or she came of age. Tameron had insisted on it, telling their kind to scatter about the fae world so they wouldn't end up in a cataclysmic fight and kill each other off like they had done in their kingdom of old: the scorpion kingdom. No one, who had known of them, knew any of them existed any longer. Well, except for the one time when the king had taken a group of fae in to learn why they were at a human Renaissance faire in their territory. Normally, they'd preferred to keep their secret…secret. They were known to be a war-like race, as if it was in their genes. But she didn't think she had the dark heart that those who fought in the wars had.

Now, she was alone in the woods, looking for a place to call home near the dragon fae territory. She knew how to build a shelter, but for now, she just wanted to take refuge from the torrential rain in a nearby cave she'd spied. Hopefully, nothing would be skulking around inside it.

She had magic skills, though she preferred using her healing skills, rather than her magic for fighting. She was afraid, if she used those skills, she might like it too much and fall down the same dark path her ancestors had taken.

She should have known what a mistake it was to enter the cave when she smelled the recent scent of a wolf. More than a wolf. Two of them. But she needed to get out of the rain. The wolves didn't. When she used her fae light, she saw only the dark cave's interior. Maybe the wolves had been here, but were now gone.

She didn't plan to go very far into the cave. Just far enough to get out of the downpour that was splashing rainwater inside. That's when she heard a low growl. Right before the brown wolf lunged at her from the shadows.

CHAPTER 2

Brett was so thrilled that Ena might be pregnant with a child of their own, that he couldn't believe any news could eclipse that. But when he saw his friend Bryan burning up with fever and looking like death-warmed over, everything else was forgotten.

"We need to get cold compresses to bring his fever down," Brett quickly said. "Do you have the flu, Bryan?"

His eyes unfocused, Bryan just stared at him as if he was delirious.

Eyes widened, Mark pointed to the covers. "There's blood on the quilt."

Alarmed, Brett moved the quilt aside and saw that Bryan's arm was sporting a vicious bite from a large animal, the area red and bleeding. "It's a defensive wound."

"We might not be able to take care of this ourselves," Ena warned.

Brett knew that taking him to a human hospital could have consequences too. He also wasn't sure that the fae could bring him back to health. Their own people were so resilient that all they needed was the help of herbs and rest, oftentimes, except for the time he was struck with two crossbow bolts. And Ena's brother had broken one of his ribs when trying to remove one of them to save his life.

"A hospital," Brett said, as Cook hurried in with cool cloths.

"Not the same one you keep going to," Ena warned. "Every time we show up there, so do the police."

"It's the closest one to our location in the fae world, but you're right. We'll have to go to another one. What bit him?" Brett breathed in the scents around the bed with his enhanced dragon smell. "Wolf?"

"You're right. Wolf. Alton has wolves guarding his treasure at Wolf Mountain. I know they live elsewhere too, but I've never heard of them entering a castle and attacking anyone. How would he have gotten in?" Ena asked.

"Unless Bryan had been outside the castle walls and was bitten," Brett said.

One of Ena's maids hurried into the chamber. "Could a wolf have taken Hannah away? I just ran in there to see if she was in her room and make sure she was okay. There are signs of wolf fur all over the bedding and the floor."

"What do we do now? If your healers can't take care

of this, we've got to get Bryan to a hospital," Mark said.

"Mark's right. A bite like that could become infected," Brett warned.

"I'm tracking down the wolf," Ena said.

Brett knew Ena would kill the wolf. The problem was the wolf could injure or kill any number of people during the rampage it was on now. Still, he thought they should talk to the leader of the wolf pack and get his help in this, if the wolf was one of his own. Simon could have a stake in this also.

"What if it was Hannah?" Muriel was wringing her hands. "What if she doesn't know how to deal with being a wolf, if she's now a wolf shifter fae?"

"Bite the hand that feeds you?" Ena said, angry.

Despite not wanting to believe Hannah was now a dangerous wolf, Muriel was right. Hannah might have found her fae abilities.

Jacob, their wheelsmith, who had been helping a lot with the gardening, since he hadn't needed to maintain wagon wheels that much, hurried into the chamber. "Ryker overheard what happened and came to get me. I can take Bryan to a hospital. Mark can come with me. I'll leave, if any fae seers suddenly show up. Since Mark and Bryan are human, no one will suspect they're one of us, in a manner of speaking."

Ryker was Ena and Brett's butler, though he often did more than that.

"What if any fae seers learn he was with you?" Ena sounded worried.

"Okay, then I can just drop the two of them off and…well, hide somewhere. But I'll be there in case they need a quick transport out of there," Jacob said.

"You can't carry two humans with you. Someone else will have to go with you," Brett said.

"You, Brett. They're your friends. You know the layout of hospitals better than any of us would. Take them, and then return when you can," Ena said.

Frowning at her, Brett took hold of her hand. "Wait for me then. Until I return. I'll help you to locate the wolf."

She shook her head. "This is what I do. I can't let a menace run wild through the kingdom."

"But you're—"

She gave him a sharp look, and he knew she didn't want the word to get out she was pregnant until she knew for sure. "I'll take Alton with me. He knows the wolves better than any of us. If the wolf is part of their pack, he can deal with Simon. If not, then he can help me track her down."

"You know for sure it's a she?" Mark asked.

Muriel nodded. "The wolf was a female. The fur she left behind is brown. So you should be looking for a brown wolf."

Brett didn't want Ena to go without him, but he knew the dark look she was giving him meant to tread lightly with what he had to say. She'd been doing things like this for a long time. He was new at it, new to their world and ways still, no matter how much he'd had to deal with dangerous situations already. Sometimes, he felt he was old hat at it, but he had only learned a little about their kind. His kind too now.

"All right, but *don't* take any risks that you shouldn't." He loved Ena with all his heart and if he lost her, he would lose part of his soul. He kissed her mouth, and then leaned over and kissed her belly before she could stop him, her face turning red with embarrassment. He hadn't meant to do it in front of her staff, particularly when they didn't know if she was pregnant or not. Well, and she wasn't for sure either.

The startled looks on their faces said it all. They knew he was worried about her…and a baby.

"Maybe, Halloran should go with you, Princess Ena," Jacob offered, as he went to lift Bryan from the bed.

Halloran was her brother, but he worked for the queen now, and Brett knew she couldn't ask him to come on this errand.

"Go! Take him to a hospital. Now." Then Ena squeezed Bryan's hand, though he didn't seem to hear or see anything that was going on. "You have too much gardening to do to die on me, human."

Mark smiled a little at her, then Brett said one last time, "Maybe—"

But her reproachful look made Brett change the topic. "We're going. Just…be careful." Then he took hold of Mark's arm, and he and Jacob and Bryan returned to the human world, but if anything happened to Ena, Brett would track down the wolf and kill her himself. No questions asked.

***

Letta threw a spark of white light at the attacking brown wolf, and it yipped. Singed fur and a curl of smoke filled the air as Letta dashed for the side of the cave to give the wolf a way out before she killed it. But the wolf attacked her, biting her arm, and Letta zapped her with a higher voltage of electricity. The wolf fell away and raced out of the cave.

It was so easy to use her spells to hurt someone, Letta thought with horror. Though she reminded herself, as a woodland fae, all she had were her magic spells to protect herself and the wolf had attacked her with wicked teeth. But what if the she-wolf had pups in the cave, a den, and it was protecting them?

Worried she might find wolf pups mewling for their momma, Letta rushed deeper into the cave to find a severely wounded gray she-wolf, her gray and blond fur with black guard hairs covered in blood. Letta realized then that the brown wolf had blood on her mouth before she'd bitten Letta. But what if this was a bad wolf and the other one was a good wolf? What if Letta saved this wolf's life, if she could, and the other wolf's pack came after her?

She didn't hesitate to throw her backpack on the floor and rummaged through it, but when she couldn't reach her medical supplies quickly enough, Letta finally dumped the contents on the floor. She grabbed a mortar, measured out herbs, and ran to the entrance of the cave to catch some of the rainwater. Then she hurried to mix the herbs with the water into a paste using a pestle as she stalked back to where the wolf lay bleeding.

"I'll patch you up in no time," Letta said, trying to comfort the wolf, if she could hear her, could smell her unique scent, and knew she wasn't a wolf, or the one who had attacked her. She began to apply a paste of the healing herbs to the wolf's wounds, and then she hurried to bandage them. "I wish you could howl for help, if you're the innocent one here. Except, I would hope they know I aided you and didn't hurt you." She ran her hand over the wolf's back where she was uninjured. "You'll make it. I'm a great healer." Though she did do well with her healing skills, this wolf was severely injured and Letta didn't know if she'd stopped her lifeforce from draining out of her body fast enough. Even if she lived, she might never be the same. Letta cast a healing chant over the wolf.

Then she took a break and applied some of the healing salve to her arm and repeated the same spell to attempt to heal her wound faster. Right before her eyes, the wound began to seal, the bleeding slowing, and she took a relieved breath. It would continue to heal until every vestige of the wound was gone. Her sleeve was bloodied and torn where the wolf had bitten her.

Letta couldn't wait for anyone to come and find the injured wolf. First, she checked deeper in the cave, just in case there was another entrance and the brown wolf came back to try and finish them both off. What she saw made her gasp. Mountains of treasure!

And that's when she realized she smelled dragon. Ohmigod, this was a dragon's lair? She was so dead meat. Had the badly injured wolf been protecting the treasure? Why would the other wolf need the treasure? Maybe it was a feud between the two wolves?

Letta hurried back to the wolf and heard the unmistakable flapping of wings. Two dragons? She thought it was bad enough that a wolf pack might find her here with the wounded wolf, but dragons finding her "stealing" their treasure? She knew there was nothing she could do to fight them, so she would have to do the next best thing: start talking in a hurry.

Two dragons. She was in serious trouble.

The male and female dragons settled on the floor in front of her, looking cross and ready to terminate her. One was olive green in color with narrowed green eyes, the female, smaller than the blue-scaled dragon, the male.

"A brown wolf attacked this one and I zapped her with an electricity spell. Not enough to kill her," she quickly said, just in case the other wolf was the good one and this one was the bad one. "I'm a healer and took care of her injuries the best I could."

Both dragons shifted and hurried to look over the injured wolf. Letta was surprised to see that the woman had her black hair cropped short, unlike most fae women who wore theirs long. And she was wearing a black leather corset and pants and thigh high boots, instead of a gown like most fae women wore. And the male looked like he'd been to the human world, dressed in a t-shirt, blue jeans, and sneakers.

"Myla," the male dragon shifter said. "Myla, can you hear me?"

When the injured wolf didn't respond, he said to the female dragon, "I'm taking her to her people. Wait here with this one, Ena. If the woman moves a muscle, take care of her."

"I didn't do this to her." Letta hated that she sounded desperate to plead her case. Then realizing they had to smell the wolf bites on Myla, and Letta couldn't have done it, she felt a little relief. Then she recalled the mountains of gold. *Great. Just great.* Now the dragons would think she knew too much about where their stash of treasure was and eliminate her!

"I'll wait. Go, Alton. Take Myla to her family," Ena said.

He shifted and lifted the wolf in his talons and flew out of the cave. Letta was glad the male dragon was gone, not that the female was any less dangerous. Letta was gladder still that the male would take Myla to her family, especially if she didn't make it through the night. She should be with her family, her pack.

Ena cocked her head to the side a little. "What kind of fae are you? I've never seen your kind before."

"Woodland fae," Letta quickly told her, as if she had something to hide. Which she did.

"Woodland fae," Ena said, her eyes narrowed. "I've never heard of such a fae."

Letta tilted her chin up, as if telling the mighty dragon shifter that she wasn't scared of her. The truth was, she was. And of the male dragon. And the wolf pack. Here she came from the mighty scorpion fae and thought she wouldn't fear anyone. Maybe after all these centuries, the dark heart of their genes no longer existed. She was afraid she'd have to toughen up if she was going to deal with the dragon shifters, when the other returned and took her to task for knowing where his treasure was.

But then Letta's healer instincts came to bear and she frowned, gazing at Ena's belly, listening for more heartbeats, and then heard them. Faint. Two. The dragon was going to have twins. Maybe this could be Letta's salvation.

"Do…you have a midwife to deliver your babies?" Though Letta had never delivered dragon fae babies before. Did they come in a shell?

***

This was going to be tough to explain, Brett thought, as Jacob carried Bryan into the hospital, and they were asked all kinds of questions about how they were going to pay for the hospitalization. Brett didn't think he'd ever have to call on Queen Viviana for anything, but he'd saved her life, and now Brett had to ask her if she'd save Bryan's.

"I'll be right back," Brett said to Mark and Jacob.

"Where—" Mark said.

"To see if Queen Viviana can pay for his hospitalization so Bryan can be seen." Brett fae traveled to the dragon fae's castle, and when he arrived, he saw Halloran, Ena's brother, and Dragon at Arms, right away. "Halloran, can I secure an urgent meeting with the queen?"

"For what purpose?" Halloran asked, as he and Brett strode toward the queen's throne room where she was having court to mete out justice for minor infractions of her laws.

"A wolf bit Bryan, but his blood is badly infected. We need hospital insurance to pay for his coverage. Viviana used to have it in the human world when she lived there. We thought, I thought, she might be able to finagle something."

"The queen does *not finagle* things." Halloran escorted him to the throne room where a courtier was pleading his case.

As soon as the queen saw Brett and Halloran, she motioned for the man to quit speaking, and called them forth.

Halloran explained the situation, and she frowned at them. "All right. I've heard he is doing an exquisite job for you with the gardens."

Brett knew Ena would have a fit if the queen wanted Bryan to work for her instead, and she'd save his life. Then again, he knew Ena would want Bryan alive and healthy, no matter where he worked.

"I will see to court upon my return, tomorrow," the

queen said, waving for a dismissal of her people. Then she followed Brett and Halloran into the hallway. She was wearing her gold crown, and a pale blue gown of silk, not her usual red gown when she was holding court. "How did Bryan injure himself so badly?"

Brett explained about Hannah, possibly being a fae wolf shifter, and biting him.

"Ena is hunting her down as we speak, I would hope," the queen said, her eyes narrowed.

"Aye, with Alton. Though I wanted to go with her."

"You're a good mate, but your friend needed you. Now he needs me. But I will require payment of his services afterward." Then Viviana abruptly switched subjects. "So, Hannah isn't a human after all."

"If the wolf fur that we found in her bedchamber is any indication, no."

"I need to change attire."

Brett was surprised that, once she had returned to the dragon fae kingdom, the queen still had human clothes to wear in their world. Then again, so did they, so when they wanted to visit the human realm, they would look the part. Not that any of the rest of them had taken the time to change out of their tunics, trewes, and thigh-high boots before going to the human world this time.

She soon joined them, wearing blue jeans, sneakers, a sweater, no crown, no fae gown. She looked like she'd fit into the human's world just fine. Mark, Jacob, Bryan, and Brett, on the other hand, looked as though they were playing a game of "Dungeons and Dragons."

CHAPTER 3

When they arrived at the hospital, Viviana didn't act like a queen. She portrayed a concerned mother, worried that her boy was going to die. Which he could.

Brett had to give her a gold star for the ultimate performance. She didn't leave it at that, but stayed with them in Bryan's hospital room. Brett couldn't have appreciated her more for it. Mark, Jacob, and Brett pretended to be Bryan's brothers. And then the cops came. Every time they ended up at a hospital, cops were called. Brett should have known when Bryan was bitten so badly that they'd want to find the dog—they couldn't say it was a wolf—and put it down before it attacked anyone else.

"Where was the dog that bit him? We need to take it down and ensure it didn't have rabies," the police officer said.

Poor Bryan was still out of it, and Brett worried they

were too late. When Brett had lived in the human world and was in Boy Scouts, his leader had died from a sinus infection, his whole body becoming infected before they could stop it. So he knew how serious this could be.

They weren't about to say it was a wolf. There were no wolves in Texas any longer. But if the hospital staff tested the bite mark, they could determine it was wolf's saliva.

Bryan's vital signs were stable, but he wasn't coming out of the coma, and that didn't bode well. Maybe he was in a vegetative state. Maybe he'd never be able to come out of this. Brett felt awful that Bryan's willingness to be with them in the fae world could come to this. That his liking Hannah could have resulted in this.

What irritated Brett was that he was a powerful mage, a dragon shifter, and yet he couldn't do anything for his friend. Mark was scowling, looking angry that he couldn't do anything for Bryan either.

"We don't know, sir. He called us and said he had been bitten and by the time we reached our home, he was already out of it," Brett lied.

"Where had he been? Did he tell you anything before he was bitten?" the officer asked.

"No. Mark and I were going to bring a pizza home later and watch a movie. By then, he'd called to say he'd been bitten. I asked where the dog was, what it looked like and said we were on our way, but he was non-responsive by that time. This is the way he was when we arrived at the house. We called Mom, and she rushed home from the mall to help us bring him to the hospital."

"You didn't call an ambulance?" the officer asked, brow raised.

"We live out in the country. Sometimes people get lost trying to reach our place," Brett said. "We just figured it was faster to bring him here ourselves."

The police officer glanced at Viviana. She nodded.

The officer snapped his notebook closed. "We'll check back with him, when he comes out of the coma. We'll need the home address."

Vivian gave him her old home address. Then the officer left the room.

Brett breathed a sigh of relief. New hospital, new police jurisdiction. The officer didn't connect the dots of who Brett was, when he'd had serious medical issues from being hit by a crossbow's bolt, two, in fact, or the sword wound Brett had suffered. Living in the fae world did have some dangerous consequences.

Once the police officer shut the door to give them some privacy, Viviana said, "Maybe this is best for him."

Mark turned his dark look on her, and she frowned at him. She was still a powerful dragon fae queen, *not* their mother. Though her look softened at once. She had lived among the humans for years. She knew the dangers they could face with a simple infection. And she knew the boys had been friends for years.

Brett gave Mark a look that said to apologize to her, but Mark only turned his worried gaze on Bryan.

The queen took a seat on a chair nearby to anxiously wait with them, her foot tapping nervously on the floor. Brett appreciated her vigilance. She could have returned home to let them deal with this on their own. She was a good queen. He knew her father, had he still been king and wasn't dead for his own treachery, would have let Bryan stay here and perish, or get better. The king wouldn't have returned Bryan to the fae world.

Then Bryan moaned, and Viviana was on her feet in a flash, moving toward the bed, Brett and Mark trying to speak with him.

"Bryan, tell us what happened," Brett said, holding his hand. "Was it Hannah who bit you? Did she turn into a wolf?"

Bryan stared at him as if he couldn't understand the question.

And then, the unthinkable happened. Right before his eyes, Bryan's body blurred and in an instant, he shifted into a snarly, gray wolf.

***

As wolves, Simon and his three brothers rushed into the cave to take care of the person who had so gravely wounded his sister, only to see Ena and a fae he didn't know. Her hair was pale blond, and her eyes blue. She looked like she was a daughter of the moon.

He was taken in by her appearance for a moment, so were his brothers, but then he snapped out of it when he smelled his sister's blood, and another wolf's, on her. He approached her, sniffed her, and realized she wasn't a wolf shifter. The other wolf that had been here had gotten away.

He shifted. "Valoran and Aegis, you search for the wolf's trail. Killington, Ronan, you guard Alton's treasure."

The other two wolves took off and Killington and Ronan stayed put.

"You are coming with me," Simon said, seizing the fae's arm. She couldn't fae transport out of the cave because of the iron ore, but he knew very well that she could, once he moved her out of the cave. "Tell me what you were doing here."

"And how you think you know about me," Ena said, hurrying after them.

Simon glanced at the dragon shifter, wondering what that was all about.

"I was looking for shelter from the rain. I smelled the wolves and hesitated to venture further into the cave, when a brown wolf came out of the dark and attacked me. I hit her with…" She hesitated to say.

Simon observed her. He figured she hadn't wanted to reveal the kinds of powers she had. But he was glad to know she hadn't been in league with the wolf, if the rogue wolf had attacked this woman also.

"With?" he growled. They needed answers, not half-truths.

"An electrical charge. I didn't kill the brown wolf, because I didn't know if she was just protecting cubs in the cave. I didn't know she had fought with another wolf.

When I saw Myla, and how badly she was injured, I knew the wolves had fought. But whose fault was it? What if the two wolves were just having a quarrel?"

"Goddess's wounds, you could have killed her! The brown wolf, I mean. Now we have to try and track her down," Simon said, irritated to high heaven with the unknown fae.

"I...didn't...know...that." The fae's face was crimson with anger. "What if Myla was the one at fault? And the other wolf was part of your pack too? And I'd killed her? Then you'd want me dead."

Simon snorted. Though he had to agree her reasoning was sound and she had tried to heal his sister. Alton wouldn't like that the fae knew where his treasure was though. Since she hadn't been there to steal from the dragon fae, Alton might let her go with a stern warning. Or not. Dragon shifters could be really prickly when it came to anyone knowing where they hid their gold. And what if the story of her trying to get out of the rain was just a ploy? What if she had suspected a dragon's treasure was in the cave? Then she came across the vicious wolf, and the other that had been badly wounded, and everything had changed?

"How do you know about me?" Ena asked again, her eyes wide.

"I...have exceptional hearing."

Simon looked at the women, expecting one of them to enlighten him, but when neither did, he heard the rain had stopped and moved the woman out of the cave.

"What's your name?"

"Letta."

"And your fae kind? I don't recognize your aura." It was a pretty, mystical silver.

"Woodland fae."

"I've never heard of them." Then he paused, his hand still on the woman's arm. "I'm Simon, and Myla is my sister. Thank you for saving her life."

"Where are you from?" Ena asked Letta.

"From the woodlands, a long way from here. It was time for me to leave."

Simon wondered if her magic had anything to do with it. "Because you're trouble?"

"Because I've come of age. Whoever comes of age has to leave the woodlands."

"I've never heard of anything that absurd," Simon said. Most fae kind stayed with their own kind for friendship, family, and safety.

Letta didn't enlighten him further.

Then Alton joined them as a dragon, settling in front of them. He shifted, narrowing his eyes at Letta. "Explain what you were doing in my cave."

The woodland fae rolled her eyes. Simon stared at her in disbelief. That was such a human reaction, he wondered if she'd lived among them for a while.

She explained all over again about what she was doing there.

Alton frowned at her. "You know you'll have to die because you know where my treasure is."

"I have a job for her," Ena said, "if she knows anything about what she says she knows."

Alton waited for Ena to explain, but she didn't say anything more. Simon suspected it was something Ena didn't want to share with anyone right this moment, which made him intensely curious as to what it was about.

"What will Brett say to that?" Alton didn't look happy that Ena planned to protect the woodland fae.

"He will be fine with it."

Simon had been surprised when Alton hadn't won Ena over to be his mate and the human Brett had instead. Though, Brett had turned out to be a dragon shifter also.

"I hold you personally responsible if the woman steals any of my treasure," Alton said, sounding like he truly didn't trust the woodland fae and that, though he was now mated, and still Ena's good friend, he'd make her pay in treasure if Letta stole his.

"Why are you here?" Simon asked Letta. "I mean, of all the places you could choose to be, why are you in this region?"

"I met Princess Alicia once. She's a dragon fae and her intended, a dark fae prince, dropped into my homeland. His cousin Micala also, and his human girlfriend. They seemed nice. I thought I could make a fresh start in the dragon fae territory because I knew Princess Alicia."

Ena's jaw dropped. Simon took that to mean Ena knew something about the woodland fae.

"I wasn't sure about living in the dark fae territory. I was trying to reach the dragon fae lands, and didn't realize this was wolf territory," Letta said.

"If you're finished with Letta," Ena said to Simon and Alton, "I'll take her home. Then I'll return and help with the search for the wolf."

"Later," Simon said.

Ena arched a brow.

Wolf Mountain territory was governed by the wolf fae. They had a nice arrangement with Alton, concerning protecting his gold, but it was *still* their territory. Alton couldn't just take over the cave on wolf lands and store his treasure there without their permission.

Simon wasn't about to give up the woodland fae either. Not just yet. She might still be useful as far as her healing powers went. Then he wondered why Ena would even be here. Alton was here, checking on his treasure, yes. Maybe Alton's mate, Kayla, would have come, but not Ena.

"Fine," Ena said, not sounding as though it was fine with her one iota. "I'll take her with me after I've finished the hunt for the brown wolf."

Simon narrowed his eyes at her. "That's why you're here? You were hunting the wolf down?"

"She bit one of the men on my staff. He's human and sick with an infection. Brett took him to the human world to one of their hospitals."

"You have to bring him back to our world," Simon said, alarmed. What a disaster that would be if he turned into a wolf while he was at the human hospital.

"Didn't you hear the part where he's sick and dying?" Ena sounded totally exasperated with him.

"The wolf fae genetics will help him to heal. Who's with him?"

"Brett and my wheelsmith, Jacob, and Bryan's human friend, Mark. I don't understand."

"They must return him at once before he turns."

"Into a wolf?" Ena was staring at Simon like he was crazy.

"Yes! We'll deal with him and teach him to be one of us. If he doesn't learn from us, he could lash out at anyone, your mate, his friend Mark, or Jacob even."

"He could turn my mate?" Ena sounded shocked to the core.

"No, but he could kill him. The wolf bite will only affect humans in that way." He glanced at Letta, and saw the blood on her sleeve, thinking it was from his sister, but he realized it wasn't his sister's or the other wolf's. Not from the scent. Which meant it had to have been Letta's. And her sleeve was torn. He pulled up her sleeve, but her skin showed no indication that she'd been bitten. He was glad for that. Not that the wolf would have turned her, but he just didn't want her to be injured also. Still, why was he smelling her blood?

"Oh, just great. I have no idea which hospital they ended up at," Ena said, breaking into his thoughts.

There was no time to delay. Simon warned her, "I strongly suggest you find him fast."

Ena nodded and vanished.

"Are you sure?" Alton asked Simon.

"Yeah. If the brown wolf hasn't been with her kind before to learn how to socialize and be one of us, she could go on a real killing spree." Simon looked down at Letta. "I'll speak to the elders of the council and see what they want to do with you." They were his advisors, but he always made the final decisions for the pack.

"I don't have to live here. I thought I was in the dragon fae territory."

"You aren't."

Alton said, "I'm looking for the rogue wolf. I'll return to see how Myla is doing later."

Simon only hoped Ena would return the human, who'd been turned, to their world before it was a disaster for everyone she cared for, and for the human population too.

***

Ena transported back to her castle, unsure as to what to do next. She didn't know where Brett and Jacob had taken Bryan exactly. They were going to a hospital she'd never been to before. She'd never lived in the human's world like some of the others had, though she'd visited it from time to time, mostly to take care of a mission—like now.

She went to see her brother at the royal castle and realized Brett had recently come here. She followed his faery dust trail to the queen's court. When she arrived there, she saw her brother Halloran and hurried to intercept him. "Do you have any idea where Brett took Bryan?"

"He took him to a hospital in the human world."

"Right, but which one?"

"I don't know. The queen went with Brett because he needed her to use her insurance to pay for Brett's hospital stay."

"Ohmigoddess, no."

Halloran frowned at his sister. "What's wrong, Ena?"

"Simon, one of the wolves of the pack at Wolf Mountain, said that if the wolf bit Bryan, he could shift and then fight any of them."

"God's wounds. Let's go." Halloran grabbed Ena's arm, and they followed Brett and the queen's fae dust trail to the hospital in the human world.

The good thing was that most of the human buildings didn't have iron ore in them, so the fae could go where they wanted to without any trouble. They found the floor where Brett and the others had gone. They finally reached the room where the fae trail led them and heard growling inside.

As soon as they threw the patient room door open, a gray wolf lunged at Ena. Her heart lurched. All she could think of was protecting her babies.

Immediately, Brett cast some kind of spell on the wolf and he sank to the floor.

So did Ena, and she was *not* the fainting type.

Halloran started barking orders, even though his

queen was hurrying to see to Ena, Brett right behind her. "Jacob, grab Bryan. We transport to Ena and Brett's castle now."

Brett gathered Ena in his arms, cursing under his breath. The queen took hold of Mark's hand so he could go with them. Jacob carried the sleeping wolf, and the whole lot of them vanished from the hospital room.

Ena imagined the police would be called again to the hospital as soon as the staff saw that their patient had…vanished. The wolf fur on the bed would be just as tough to explain.

CHAPTER 4

"Did anyone else get bitten?" Halloran asked the gathered fae at Ena and Brett's castle: the dragon fae queen, Ena, Brett, Jacob, and Mark.

They had locked a sleeping Bryan, still in his wolf form, in one of the cells in the dungeon where Ena and Brett stored their treasure. But it was the only place where he'd be secure at the castle.

Brett was sitting on a couch in the common area of his and Ena's castle, his arm around Ena. She still looked pale, and he wondered if that had all to do with the baby she was carrying. He was certain now that she was. He'd never seen her faint before, and he was sure she wasn't happy that anyone else saw her so indisposed either.

"No, as soon as he jumped from the bed, we were talking to him, trying to reason with him to reach him. We didn't know if he understood who we were even," Brett said. "Did you find the brown wolf?"

"She tore into one of the wolves who guards Alton's treasure," Ena said. "A woodland fae took care of Myla and used some kind of spell on the brown wolf to stop her from attacking her. The wolf ran off. Simon's brothers and Alton are searching for her. But he said Bryan needs to live with them, to learn how to be one of them. Otherwise, he could be a wild wolf, killing people indiscriminately all over the place."

"Like the brown wolf, if it's Hannah," Brett said.

"If she had been left in the human world, she could have created real havoc," the queen said. "It makes me wonder if we shouldn't start capturing the fae seers and let them live here until they change, if *they* change. If not, they're stuck in our world as humans. Or, we can return them to their world, if the years pass and they don't become one of us."

"I'm not taking in any more humans," Ena said.

"She can't," Ryker said. Ena's butler sometimes served as her advisor, and he always had Ena's best interest at heart. "Not when she's got a little one on the way."

Ena scowled at him.

"It's true, isn't it?" Ryker shook his head. "She can't take in any more humans. Not when they can cause all this trouble."

The queen smiled at Ena. "I'm so happy for you, dear. Our first little baby dragon shifter in years."

"I haven't had it confirmed, yet. Ryker is speaking out of turn."

"I'll send my physician to see you at once. If Ena doesn't have any objection, I think it best if we do what Simon suggests. Turn Bryan over to the wolf pack of Wolf Mountain."

Mark looked devastated.

"He'll return here, Mark," Ena said. "He's family, even if he's a wolf shifter fae now. And you need help with the gardens."

"About that," the queen said.

Everyone looked at her, waiting to see what she had to say.

She shrugged and smiled. "I had a deal with Brett that he'd have Bryan work for me on my gardens, once I paid for his medical expenses to save his life. But if that's not possible, I'll have Mark do the work instead. Not all the work. He can plan the gardens, and my people will create them."

Mark agreed to it, not that he had any other choice.

"And for that, I'll convey the title of Royal Master Gardener on you."

Mark smiled.

"Let me know what happens to the brown wolf." Then the queen headed for the castle door and Ryker hurried to open it for her, with all the aplomb of a royal butler, since Brett and Ena were now royals too.

"How long will the sleeping spell work on Bryan?" Ena asked Brett.

"A few hours, more or less, depending on his ability to fight it," Brett said.

"Do you really think it's a good idea to leave him with a pack of wolves?" Mark asked. "What if he fights them, and they feel they have no alternative but to kill him?"

"We pray that it doesn't happen," Ena said. "But we can't have a wild wolf at the castle, putting everyone here at risk. And we can't keep him locked up forever."

"My apologies for mentioning your condition in front of the queen," Ryker said, returning to the common area.

Ena frowned at him.

Ryker shrugged, not looking in the least apologetic. "Now the queen is sending her—"

There was a knock at the door.

"Physician to learn the truth. Which means Cook will need to prepare special foods for you and the baby."

Ena scowled at him, not wanting her household to be in an uproar over the baby, or babies, if Letta was right. "She does not."

Ryker hurried to get the door, opened it, and said, "Do come in. The princess awaits you in the common room."

"My bedchamber," Ena corrected him, and Brett took her to their chamber, though she gave him a look like he'd better not even think of coddling her over this. She was a fierce dragon fae shifter, after all.

***

Brett thought Ena might dismiss him from their chamber when the queen's physician examined her, but she didn't. *He* about fainted when he learned they were going to have twins in the spring, not just *a* baby.

Ena smiled at Brett, and then frowned. "That doesn't mean I'm giving up working on missions until the babies arrive. Oh, and, though I don't know her qualifications, the woodland fae who saved Myla's life, at least I hope she did, said she could be my midwife."

The queen's physician shook his head. "We haven't had dragon shifter babies in so long, I would be honored and remiss if I didn't deliver them."

"All right. But Letta will watch over me in the meantime."

Seeming pleased that he would get to deliver her babies, the physician bowed his head, smiling.

Brett didn't think Ena meant it. She didn't need anyone watching over her. He suspected, for whatever reason, she was on a new mission to save the woodland fae. Another misfit to join their ranks?

"You are sure she is safe to have around?" Brett asked. Now that they were going to have two new members of the family, Brett wanted to ensure they were well-protected.

"No, but everyone can keep an eye on her."

The physician gave Ena a list of things she should and shouldn't do during the various stages of pregnancy, then he bowed to them, and left.

Brett wanted to see the list, but Ena quickly perused it and stuck it down her bodice. He smiled at her. He would learn what the queen's physician said she could do or not do, with or without her cooperation.

They heard shouts of glee and Brett smiled. "Sounds like your staff—"

"Our staff."

"Our staff likes the news."

She sighed. "I don't want anyone making a big fuss about this."

Then someone knocked on the door and Brett knew it was Ryker from his firm knock. "Yes, Ryker."

"Halloran is here to see Ena."

She groaned. "I hope this is not about the babies. I want some normalcy around here for the next few months."

Brett helped Ena from the bed, and they went to the door.

Halloran was looking like one proud uncle, grinning from ear to ear. "You beat Alton out!"

"Oh, for heaven's sake. This is not a contest." Ena brushed past him.

Halloran slapped Brett on the back. "For being only human, as far as we all knew, you sure have made an impact on our kind."

"I thought maybe you and the falcon fae were becoming an item."

"Nah. I was just teasing her about her locket. She needed to be with her own kind." Then Halloran looked serious. "Queen Viviana said that Bryan must be handed over to the wolf pack at Wolf Mountain. I want to go with you when you do it. I assume, because you have magical skills and you're his friend, you'll want to do it."

"Yes. I welcome your company. I don't want Ena to go though."

Ena was already below stairs, so she didn't hear what he'd said, but Brett was serious. He didn't want her getting into the middle of this wolf mess in case Bryan woke and went crazy again.

"I agree. Let's do this."

Brett hoped it wasn't a mistake to take Bryan to the Wolf Mountain territory. But he hoped they would be able to help him cope with all the changes he was going through. Brett knew Mark would miss Bryan. All of them would.

When they reached the common area, all of Ena's staff was surrounding her, tears in their eyes, except for Jacob and Ryker. But the ladies were all thrilled. Of course, so were the men. They'd be the babies' protectors, no matter the cost.

Mark wasn't there with the others and Brett suspected he was in the dungeon, checking on Bryan.

"We're taking Bryan to Wolf Mountain," Brett said.

"I'm going with you," Ena said.

Halloran objected first. "He's dangerous, Ena. You have the babies to think of."

"I want to check on Letta. She's supposed to be a midwife, if she was being honest with me. I want her turned over to me."

"The queen's physician is delivering the babies," Halloran said.

"He agreed that Letta could be there also. Mark is down in the dungeon seeing Bryan. Let's go."

Brett knew from the way Ena was looking so stubborn, he didn't stand a chance of talking her out of going. Truth be told, that was part of the reason he loved her. She was protective of those who needed protection, despite her dragon persona of been tough to the scales.

When they reached the dungeon, Mark was reaching through the bars, petting Bryan, talking to him, consoling him.

"No!" Brett said, and instantly, Bryan snapped and snarled, and Mark jerked his hand through the bars, but too late.

"Did he break the skin?" Ena asked, angered. "You were supposed to work on the gardens, and you even became the queen's Royal Master Gardener. Now this!"

Halloran folded his arms and shook his head.

Brett examined Mark's bite wound. "Yeah, he broke the skin. I don't know if it means you'll shift for sure, but we'll leave both of you with the wolves for a time. What were you thinking?" Though Brett knew Mark was only concerned about his friend and was offering him comfort.

"That he was scared in there. Wouldn't you be?" Mark said, though he was furious sounding, he also sounded worried.

"Yeah. But at least when I turned into a dragon, I knew I could protect Ena," Brett said.

She snorted. "Look what that got you."

"Two bolts in the side. I know, but I *did* protect you." Brett cast a spell to put Bryan back to sleep. "Okay, who's taking whom this time?"

"I'll take Mark," Halloran said. "I'm not sure I trust your sleeping spell all that well."

"Yeah, but what if Mark turns on you?" Ena said, sounding worried about her brother's safety.

"He *can't* hurt a dragon."

***

Simon wasn't sure what to do about Letta, though he didn't want her ill-treated after she had saved his sister's life. The easiest thing to do would be to let her go to live with Ena and her staff. She didn't belong among the wolves.

But when Brett arrived with a sleeping gray wolf, Halloran had brought another human with him. Halloran was Dragon at Arms, so Simon wondered why he was even here. And Ena had come too. Simon was afraid that she was going to insist that Letta go back with her.

The wolf council wanted Letta here for now. They wanted to know more about what kind of fae she was and about the place she was from. They always had to be careful about mystery fae and their true intentions. She could be a scout for her kind, for all they knew, looking for a new place for her kind to settle.

Letta was in Myla's cottage, seeing to her. She seemed genuinely worried about her, maybe about her own fate too.

"What are you doing here?" Simon asked Halloran,

his gaze taking in the human. And then he saw his bloody hand. "No."

"Yeah," Halloran said. "I hope you can manage two of them."

Simon shook his head. "Yeah, but we need to take that other wolf down."

Then Ena said, "Where's Letta?"

"In the hut with Myla."

"I need to see her."

"She's in that hut."

Ena stalked off that way, and Bryan stirred in Brett's arms. "Have you got a secure place for them? Can they be together, or would it be less dangerous if they each have their own cage?"

"Separate. We don't know how they'll react toward each other, any more than we'll know how they'll react to the rest of us. Cages are over there, and I suggest you put them each in one. *Now*."

CHAPTER 5

At the healer's hut, Letta was feeling awfully strange, *just* where she'd been bitten. Though the wound appeared healed—it was itching. She'd never experienced anything like it after healing a wound. Usually, she felt no after-affects at all. And it wasn't just her skin, but deep beneath the skin. She worried that she'd turn into a wolf next. How awful! She liked the beauty of the wolves, when they weren't trying to kill her, but she really didn't want to be one of them.

Simon glanced over at her and frowned. "What's wrong?"

She looked out the window at the wolf and the human in the large cages, tall enough to accommodate a man standing six-foot-four. A large mat and bedding filled part of the cage. She sure didn't want to be locked up in one, if they thought she might turn. But Simon had said that fae couldn't be changed. Still, she was feeling awfully lightheaded all of a sudden. She didn't feel herself at all.

One minute, she was standing, and the next she was in Simon's arms, and she had no idea how that had happened.

"Is she feverish?" Ena asked, sounding concerned.

"Yes. But I can't leave her in the healer's hut. Not if she turns into a wolf." Simon sounded worried about her and about his sister. "I don't want to kill Letta after she saved my sister's life, but I will, to protect my sister and the pack. Family means everything to us."

"No one's killing her. I'll take her home to my castle to recover," Ena said.

"No," Brett said.

Ena gave him a murderous look. Letta took that to mean Ena didn't like her mate telling her what she was going to do. Good for her.

"Not when our babies could be at risk," Brett said, trying to reason with her.

Okay, Ena's mate had a point.

Ena said to Simon, "I thought you told us that a wolf bite couldn't affect a fae."

"There's never been a documented case of it. Our people normally don't bite humans either. But the brown wolf hasn't been raised with our kind from birth, if what we suspect is true. That she is the human who had been staying at your castle," Simon said. "Then again, we don't *really* know what Letta is. A fae kind none of us have heard of?"

"Letta is burning up with fever, just like Bryan was," Brett warned Ena.

Then they heard another wolf snarling.

Simon glanced out the window. "Mark, the other human who was bitten just turned. Letta goes in a cage."

If Letta could have used her magic, she would have zapped the wolf holding her in his arms. Though he'd probably drop her and that wouldn't help her. She felt she didn't have any energy to do anything but just lie there.

"Brother," Myla said, finally coming to, and Letta was afraid Simon would drop her to go to his sister. "She saved my life."

Simon looked down at Letta as if he hadn't already known that, or he needed to be reminded. "I'll be back."

Letta knew he was going to put her in a cage. And he was going to do it himself.

Ena hurried after him, and Letta thought she had a real advocate in the dragon fae. "I'll take her home with me," Ena insisted.

"No," both Brett and another man said, hurrying after them.

"Halloran," Ena said, "butt out. And, Brett—"

"You have no say in the matter, Ena," Simon said, his voice stern. "She was caught trespassing in our cave, on our land—"

"And saved your sister's life." Ena folded her arms across her waist.

"She very well could be one of us," Simon finished. "Go home. I've got this under control."

"She's feverish," Ena said.

"If she turns, she'll overcome the fever," Simon said.

Letta didn't think he knew that for sure, especially since he didn't think a wolf could turn one of the fae.

Ena looked at Mark and Bryan in the cages. Mark was growling and biting at the cage bars. Bryan was sitting on his furry butt, looking sad, his head down. He glanced at Brett as if, since he was his friend, he would be his salvation.

Letta knew Simon wouldn't budge on his decision. She just hoped Myla would get well fast and could help her out, if Letta was stuck in a cage and was lying there dying of a fever. Sure, their fae healing genetics could usually make them heal faster, but she had no idea how this would affect her long-term, if she managed to live through it.

She never thought taking refuge in a cave to get out of the rain could lead to this.

Then it began to rain again. On top of them.

"If you put her in a cage in the rain while she's feverish, and you don't even know for sure that she's going to turn into a wolf...," Ena growled.

Letta appreciated Ena for sticking up for her.

Simon moved Letta back into the healer's hut and laid her on a bed. Ena had followed him inside. He looked like he was torn about what to do next.

Letta would have smiled if she hadn't been in such a bind. She closed her eyes and let them work it out among themselves, hoping she wasn't going to be caged, sitting out in the rain.

"Move the wolves to a dry hut," Simon called out, not moving from where he stood next to Letta.

She suspected he was afraid to leave her alone with the dragon fae, not so much that she might harm his sister. If Ena wanted to, she could turn into her dragon and carry Letta off. That's what Letta figured he was afraid of.

Halloran and Brett joined them in the healer's hut.

"They're settled in a hut where it's nice and warm and dry with fresh dry bedding. Mark's calmed down," Brett said. "We promised them we'd find Hannah, if that's who it was that attacked Myla, Letta, and Bryan."

Ena was glowering at Simon. He wasn't backing down. He was too alpha for that, Letta thought. Ena wasn't backing down either. She was just as alpha.

"Please, Ena," Brett said, taking her hand, and kissing it. "Simon and the others will take care of Letta. We'll return here after we've searched for the brown wolf. We have the advantage of soaring high above the forest and seeing the smallest movement way down below."

"You and I need to talk," Ena said to Brett, and Letta assumed they were not going to have pleasant words. To Letta, she said, "I will be back to check on you."

Letta said, "Thanks."

Then Ena left the hut, Brett followed, and Halloran eyed Letta for a moment before leaving, frowning at her, then followed the others out. Once they heard the flapping sound of the three dragons leaving the area, Simon lifted Letta into his arms—at least he was gentle in his actions—then he carried her into the hut where the other two wolves were staying. And right across the hut from them sat a nice, large cage, just for her. And another one that was empty that she assumed was for Hannah, if they didn't kill her outright when they found her.

Letta figured Simon wouldn't let any dragon tell him what to do. Not unless it had to do with guarding Alton's gold. Other than that, the dragon fae had no say in how they ruled their own lands.

Simon carried Letta into the cage, then set her down on the bed someone had made for her.

"If you shift, don't tear up your bedding," he warned her. "It's all you've got."

She wondered why he'd think she'd tear up her bedding! She wasn't a wild beast.

"Wolves tend to scratch at their bedding when they're wolves to make it theirs and more comfortable. Just saying."

Great.

He locked the cage. "Our healer will see to you in a little bit."

Then he left her with the wolves and she could have growled she was so angry. And she wasn't even a wolf!

***

Simon returned to the healer's hut to see his sister. She was scowling at him. It seemed he was at odds with everyone right now, but he wouldn't put her life, or any of the other wolves' lives in the pack, at risk because they didn't know what would happen to Letta.

Myla told their healer, "Go see to the fae. I'm fine." She was still lying on the bed, her wounds covered in bandages. She looked paler than he'd ever seen her. "You said a wolf couldn't change a fae. Make up your mind," Myla snapped at Simon.

"She's running a fever, like the humans had done before they shifted. She was bitten by the she-wolf, like the one human had been," Simon said.

Myla scoffed. "She's a fae."

Simon stared out the door at the rain. "A mystery fae. A woodland fae! There is no such thing. She lies. Why did she really come here?" He turned to face his sister.

"Certainly, not to see you. Or to be attacked by one of our kind. Why don't you go help the others look for the wolf?"

Simon let out his breath in exasperation. "I'm watching over you."

"You are doing nothing of the sort. I'm fine. Are you afraid the brown wolf will tear into you like she did me, if you find her?"

Simon growled. The very idea. "All right. I'll go. But I want you to stay right in that bed and do whatever the healer tells you to do."

"Of course. Do I look like I want to leave the bed?"

No. His sister might be resting there, talking, ordering him about, but she still looked like it would take some time for her to heal.

He sighed. "I'll return soon." Truth be told, he did want to take care of the brown wolf, one way or another. Sitting here babysitting Letta and his sister wasn't his idea of fun, especially when his sister was just as annoyed with him. Then he shifted and ran out the door as a wolf. He hoped he could get this done soon. He wanted to take the wolf down before she hurt anyone else.

He returned to Alton's cave of treasure, then followed the brown wolf's scent from there.

He smelled a lot of wolves' scents who belonged to the pack: his two brothers that he'd sent after the wolf, and others who had gotten word that the wolf had injured his sister and chased after her on their own.

Way up above, he saw the dragons circling, looking for any sign of the wolf. He wanted to kill her for nearly killing his sister, but he reminded himself the wolf hadn't been herself and hadn't learned their ways. He still wanted to kill her. She was just lucky his sister was recovering.

***

Letta was lying down on the mattress, feeling horrible. Her whole body ached, and she felt feverish, then chilled. She drew a blanket over her and then saw a woman coming into the hut. She was the healer, who had been caring for Myla.

"I'm here to see to your needs," the older woman said. She eyed Letta with the wisdom of an older wolf.

"I'm coming into the cage. Please don't shift and tear into me like the other wolf did Myla."

Letta shook her head. "I'm just feverish and chilled, not turning into a furry wolf."

The woman didn't look reassured but opened the cage and walked inside. She shut the cage door but couldn't lock it while she was inside.

Letta did have the notion of rushing past the healer and making her escape, but that was all she did. *Thought* about it. She was aching too much to get up and do anything. Besides, if the wolves found her, they might kill her, thinking she was going to be too much trouble.

Still in their wolf forms, Mark and Bryan were now laying down in their cages, heads on paws, watching them. She wondered when they'd turn back into their human forms. Or were they fae now? She guessed they were. If they had been a different type of fae, and their bodies still hadn't taken on the new fae form, why hadn't their bodies blocked the wolf change? She was beginning to think Simon didn't know what he was talking about and any fae, who wasn't a wolf shifter, could be turned by a wolf fae if bitten.

Except...except she hadn't changed. How long had it taken for the humans to turn? Then again, maybe, because she was a fae, it was taking longer to affect her. Maybe her body was fighting it, even though she couldn't feel that it was.

Then she saw Myla coming into the hut. "Oh, you should be in bed," Letta said, thinking the poor woman looked ill to the bone.

"I wanted to see how you are doing, and I wanted to thank you personally for saving my life," Myla said.

"Why are you up and about?" The healer sounded annoyed. "You will undo all the good I've done, well, and that Letta has done for you."

Myla entered the cage. "Have you had any urge to shift?" she asked Letta, ignoring the healer.

"What would the urge feel like?" Letta asked. "Except for being hot, then cold and achy all over, I don't feel anything else."

"Okay, your muscles will stretch. You won't feel anything but a warm sensation filling every pore. It won't hurt. And then you'll shift in a flash. Just like that." Myla snapped her fingers. "Just a beautiful blurring of forms."

"I don't feel anything like that. Just tired, and all the rest."

"Okay, well, I'll return to bed and check on you again as soon as I can. I feel like that myself. Thanks again for saving my life. Even though I couldn't open my eyes, or respond, I heard you talking to me, and I so appreciated you fighting the wolf and taking care of my injuries."

Letta barely heard what Myla was saying, because in that instant, she was feeling really strange. And before she knew it, she was sitting on the mat as a wolf. Not that she could see herself in such a bizarre way, but she could see she had furry forelegs that had taken the place of her arms, and she was sitting on a furry behind.

"Back out slowly," Myla said to the healer.

"I'm backing out," the healer said, a quaver in her voice.

But Letta didn't feel in the least bit feral, not like the humans had reacted. She was still feeling feverish, worn out, and so she laid down on the bedding. The healer had backed out of the cage, but Myla was standing near the entrance, watching Letta.

Myla was frowning at Letta. "I don't think she's going to react like the humans who were turned."

"Maybe because she's a fae. But maybe she will change her mind and come after us. Please, Myla, come out of there now so we can shut and lock the door."

"You won't hurt me, will you?" Myla approached Letta.

Letta knew that with animals, if they showed their belly, they were indicating their subservience. Not that she wanted to pretend being subservient to anyone, but she wanted to show Myla she had no intention of harming her. She rolled over on her belly, legs stretched out, tail sweeping across her mattress in a friendly wag. She even closed her eyes, as if she were one relaxed wolf.

Myla approached her then. "Don't bite me or my brother will kill you."

Letta knew Myla was serious. She glanced at Myla and wagged her tail even harder. This was a lot more work and wearing than she thought it would be. She just wanted to sleep. She didn't have any urge to do anything else, but sleep. Though she did feel a strange urge to make her bedding more comfortable, and then she thought of Simon's words to her to not scratch at her bedding.

Myla was being careful not to scare Letta and she appreciated the wolf shifter's concern. The healer's brown eyes were wide with worry.

Myla reached Letta and crouched down to pet her. Letta rolled over onto her side, and Myla smelled like fear, but even so, she stayed put and rubbed Letta's head. "We're going to get along just fine," Myla said. "We'll be the best of friends." She smiled. Then she frowned. "I'm afraid my brother is going to give you a hard time. Just don't bite him and everything will be fine."

A man came into the hut and gasped. "Myla!"

"We're fine. I'm leaving. Just don't upset her. Letta is doing fine." Then Myla ran her hand over Letta's head again. "Sleep well, Letta. I'll return later to see how you're doing."

Then Letta closed her eyes, glad she'd made a friend in the wolf pack. Ohmigoddess, she realized what a mistake she'd made in telling them she had met Princess Alicia of the dragon fae and the others, and that's why she had come here though.

What if they talked to them and learned that Letta was a scorpion fae? And thought she could cause real trouble for them?

CHAPTER 6

Simon had been searching everywhere for the brown wolf and it was getting dark, though as a wolf, he could still see well. The same was true of the dragons, as far as their night vision went. Some of his men were still searching the woods for the wolf. Others had returned to check on the wolves in the cages and to see if Letta had turned. He wanted to return himself in the worst way and check on his sister also, but he needed to capture the menacing, brown wolf and put an end to this.

What he hadn't expected to find was the scent of the wolf heading into the cliffs. A wolf couldn't climb them. A mountain goat, yes. Or a person, maybe. He shifted and started to make the climb, then he saw a cave about twenty feet above him. He didn't know what to expect to find. A bloodthirsty wolf? Or a human or fae now, in the fae form.

He hoped she didn't attack him when he was just

making his way into the cave before he could shift. If she did, he was grabbing hold of her and taking her with him off the edge of the cliffs. She wouldn't hurt anyone ever again.

Then he heard crying inside the cave. She was in the cave, much deeper, so he thought he could still shift before she did and attacked him. When he finally breached the cave, he saw a blond-haired girl sitting on the cave floor, her arms around her knees as she sobbed. She was wearing only a nightgown and shivering in the cold cave. He needed to get the dragons' help. They could carry her down to the base of the cliffs easier than he could. And if she shifted in the meantime, she couldn't injure them.

He called out to the dragons. "Here! Over here! Inside the cave. She's returned to her fae form!" He hoped the dragons were still circling near enough to hear him, though they had exceptional hearing just like the wolves did.

Then he turned back to the woman, hoping she hadn't shifted and was coming after him. But she was just sitting there still, looking lost and unsure of herself. "I'm Simon, and from what I understand, you're Hannah?"

She nodded, her eyes glistening with tears.

"Okay, listen, you're a fae wolf shifter. Like I am. Like my sister Myla is. You injured her badly. For whatever reason, you finally came into your ability. You bit the human named Bryan, and you turned him. Then he bit Mark. Now the two of them are wolves and are just as growly as you were."

"I'm...I'm sorry. I couldn't control myself at all. I...I just had to get away from everyone, from everything, until I could control the...the beast in me. I took refuge in the cave and I guess Myla thought I was a threat and was planning to steal the gold. She attacked me first. I just reacted."

"The wolf is not a beast. It's part of who we are. The wolf. We have the enhanced abilities of sight and sound, taste and touch. You'll learn to live with it and we'll help you. My pack and I. You also bit another fae, a woodland fae. Letta. Why did you bite her?"

"She was standing in my way. I had to escape the cave and run far away. I lunged at her, meaning only to make her get out of my way, but the next thing I knew, I'd clamped my teeth down on her arm. I could have broken it. I didn't. I tasted blood, she zapped me with a taser-like light, and then I was out of there. I'd run for a long time as a wolf, saw the cliffs, and thought about climbing up them to the cave above. Then, then...I suddenly was back to the way I was before, and I climbed the cliff to seek refuge in this cave, praying that no other wolves were in here. How is Letta and your sister doing?"

"Letta shouldn't turn, but she's feverish from your bite. My sister is doing better."

"Or you would have killed me. Go ahead. I don't want to feel so out of control like this. I don't want to hurt people."

"We'll help you to learn to control it." Simon couldn't believe he was saying that to the young woman. Not after what she had done to his sister. "All right? Come with us and we'll put you up in our village." In a cage, of course. They couldn't trust that she wouldn't go on another rampage.

She didn't move from her spot of rocky floor. Then he heard flapping and she looked alarmed.

Ena entered the cave and shifted. "I ought to flame you right now for what you did to Bryan and Myla. Letta too."

That wasn't what Simon thought Ena would say. He was trying to convince the woman to go with them so they wouldn't have any trouble with her before they imprisoned her.

Halloran and Alton entered the cave next, Brett following.

The three men shifted. Brett asked, "So is she going to stay like this for a while?"

"Your guess is as good as mine," Simon said. Everyone looked at him, and he was certain they realized what he intended to do with her. "If one of you can carry her to the village, I will be grateful."

"I will," Ena said.

"No! I want *him* to carry me." Hannah pointed to Brett.

Simon didn't think that either Ena or Brett appreciated her demanding tone.

"I'll take her," Halloran said, as if he was trying to avoid his sister and her mate having issues over this later.

Halloran didn't wait for Hannah to agree, just shifted, grabbed her arms in his talons, and flew out of the cave. That's what Simon liked to see, action, but then he wanted to make sure that she was incarcerated right away. "I need her to be locked in a cage, just like the others."

"We'll make sure she is." Brett shifted and flew off.

Ena frowned at Simon, then shifted and took off after her mate.

Simon realized he should have asked one of them if they would be kind enough to carry him to the village. Now, it would take him twice as long. There was too much iron ore in the rocks which disabled his ability to fae transport.

Climbing down, he finally reached the bottom of the cliff, shifted, and howled, to let the other men know to quit searching for the brown wolf and return home.

Resounding howls rent the air and the wolves hurried to return to the village. They joined up with Simon below the cliffs. He led the pack and they finally reached home. Intending to check on Myla first, he hurried into the healer's hut to find his sister wasn't there. Neither was the healer. Now what? Had Myla gone home to their cottage?

He went to the hut where the cages were to check on the newly turned wolves and couldn't believe his eyes. His sister was sleeping beside a wolf in Letta's cage.

"What is going on here?" he demanded.

Inside the cage, the healer was sitting on a mat nearby. "Your sister and Letta have become fast friends and are sleeping."

As if he couldn't see that part. What he wanted to know was why the two of them were in there with a recently turned wolf! "I want the both of you out of there now."

"We are fine. When Letta turned into the wolf, she was totally subservient. Not once did she act growly in any way. It's as though she's always been one of us. I don't believe you need to worry about her. I'm staying here also, to ensure they're both feeling okay through the night though."

Simon couldn't believe it. He glanced around the hut and saw that Hannah had indeed been locked up in a cage also. At least his command was honored with regard to her. She was sleeping on her mat as a fae. Mark and Bryan had shifted into their wolf forms—Bryan, more of a reddish-colored wolf, and Mark had a gray, black and tan coat—and were watching them from their mats.

"What are you going to do with Hannah?" Ena asked.

"That remains to be seen." Simon wasn't going to speculate about anything any further, not after seeing the girl crying in the cave, and his sister sleeping beside Letta, the wolf. He wanted to learn the truth—had Hannah acted in self-defense at every turn? If so, there was hope for her yet.

"Then we're going home now," Ena said, Brett and Halloran agreeing.

They said goodbye to Mark and Bryan, and then left.

Simon was glad they left so he could do what he felt he had to next. It would be bad enough that the rest of his pack would learn of it.

He entered the cage, closed the door, and shifted, taking guard watch over his sister and the healer, in the event Letta woke and became dangerous. He didn't want to assign any of the men to the task because he wanted to be the one responsible for how he handled her.

Then he thought about how she knew Princess Alicia. He would pay her a visit tomorrow and learn the truth about who the fae was.

***

Ena was so angry with Brett for challenging her when she wanted to do something for Letta, and she was ready to explode when they arrived home. Her brother had come with them and she suspected he wanted to protect her mate!

Brett instantly pulled Ena into his arms and hugged and kissed her.

Ryker belatedly came to greet them, the rest of the staff already asleep. Brett shook his head at him, telling him wordlessly to return to bed. Ryker turned and headed back to his chamber.

Halloran didn't say a word, just waited to see if he was needed.

Ena finally relaxed in Brett's arms, feeling weary all

of a sudden. She didn't know why she was feeling so…emotional over practically nothing. They took turns deciding things, they always had since Brett had become her mate. She knew she was being unreasonable, yet she couldn't help herself.

Brett ran his hand over her back and kissed her again. "It's the babies."

She frowned up at him.

"I watch TV. Or I did when I was a human and living among the humans. Women would become unbal…uhm, emotional."

It was a good thing he hadn't called her unbalanced!

"It's nothing that you can control, and you love to be in control. It has to do with hormones." Brett smiled at her. "I love you, and we'll get through the mood swings. I'll always love you."

She sighed. If that's all it was, she felt better about it. "Okay, I'll work harder at trying to control my temper."

Halloran folded his arms. "Thank the goddess for that."

"Go home, brother," Ena snapped.

He smiled, bowed, and quickly exited the castle.

Brett locked the door, then took Ena to bed.

"I want to see Princess Alicia tomorrow," she said, snuggling with Brett in bed.

"You know, you are a princess now and you no longer need to call her one. She is your equal."

"She is the crown princess and will someday be

queen."

Brett sighed. "True, but she has accepted you as an equal, and for our kind that's really important."

"Okay, agreed. I'm sorry for snapping at you earlier. You are just as obstinate as I am about doing things your way, and I realize how unreasonable I was when Letta could have injured any of us. Not just you or me, or the babies even, but the rest of our staff also, if we had brought her home with us and she couldn't control her wolf. I want to check on Mark, Bryan, and Letta tomorrow too to see their progress though."

"Not Hannah?"

"She has always been a disagreeable human; now she's a disagreeable fae wolf. I can't imagine her being anything other than contrary."

Brett rubbed her arm. "You do remember we have a mission: find the prized goat before it perishes."

Ena groaned. Unless she was on another mission, which she had been, she never left her work undone.

"I could do it while you're talking to Alicia."

Ena considered it for a second, then shook her head. "Then when you found the goat, you would get the credit and all the treasure for it."

He laughed.

It was a standing joke between them because all her treasure was his and all his was hers. They piled it all in the dungeon and loved to go down there together to count it from time to time. They were dragon shifter fae after all.

"Okay, what if I fly over there tomorrow first thing and talk to her, and then meet back here to see to the goat. And, darn, I needed to tell the queen that Mark won't be working for her after all," Ena said.

"Halloran will tell her and there was nothing that could be done about it," Brett said.

"I love you, Brett."

"I love you right back," Brett said, and she knew he meant it with all his heart. Just as she did with him.

Tomorrow, she'd learn just what kind of fae Letta was, and then she and Brett would be on their way together to search for the special goat. But they'd see Brett's friends too, Letta, and Myla. And yes, Hannah, too.

***

Letta woke with a start, surprised to see she was in a cage and a wolf was sleeping nearby, when it all came back to her. She'd been bitten by a wolf, turned by the wolf, and had fallen to sleep as one. Right now, she was back to her fae self, thankfully, and alone with Simon, the wolf. Why was he in her cage? She couldn't hurt anyone here, not locked away like she was. She vaguely remembered how Myla had even slept with her for a little while. Letta couldn't appreciate her more for her kindness.

She glanced at the others in their cages also. They were all sleeping as wolves. She was glad she was back to her normal self.

Simon lifted his head and his eyes widened. She

suspected he was surprised she'd shifted.

"I'm hungry. When can I eat?" Letta folded her arms and looked cross at him.

Simon glanced in the direction of the other cages and saw all the sleeping wolves. He shifted into his fae form. "Shift for me."

She sighed. She didn't want to be a wolf.

"Try. Think of being a wolf."

She *didn't* want to be a wolf!

"You don't have any control over the shifting then," he said, baiting her.

Then she realized what he was getting at. If she couldn't control her shifting, she couldn't be let out of the cage. Then she was getting out of here for good. She'd find somewhere else to live.

She concentrated on shifting and turned into her wolf and he smiled. Really smiled. She thought he had a handsome smile, for being a brigand. Then she realized he hadn't shifted into his wolf to attack her in the event she attacked him.

"Shift back," he said.

He was so unbelievably bossy! But she'd do it because she wanted to be fae, not a wolf. She shifted and folded her arms. "Enough! I'm hungry."

"Shift again."

She frowned. "No! Feed me first."

"Shift."

She figured he would never let her out of here unless she shifted a million times for him. She noticed the other wolves were sitting up, watching them now.

She shifted back and forth five more times, not waiting for him to tell her to do it. She was tired of him telling her what to do. She was a powerful scorpion fae after all. When she was a fae again, she folded her arms...*again.*

He smirked. "Willful fae. I'll be back."

He exited the cage and locked the door. She couldn't believe it! It had been unlocked all night? And she could have slipped away while he was snoozing? She could have screamed. Or shifted and growled. She didn't want to eat in the cage! Hadn't she proved she could shift at will now?

Simon left the hut and the one in the cage named Hannah shifted.

It looked like Hannah had her shifting under control too, but she hadn't wanted to prove it to Simon. Letta didn't blame her, though it could afford Letta some freedom, she was hoping.

"So you were living in the human world, a fae seer, before Ena brought you here?" At least that's what Letta thought from the conversation she'd overheard.

"What's it to you?" Hanna snapped.

Oh, my. Letta was ready to zap with her magic her again, except using a little more strength this time. "We're both caged here, so it would be nice to know who the goddess bit me and put me in this predicament."

Hannah smiled a little at that, and her smile wasn't in the least bit friendly. More so that Hannah was glad that she had done it. "You were in my escape path. Myla had already attacked me, protecting the treasure from an unknown wolf. It stoked my ire and I tore into her. I didn't know my own strength. Then I made a hasty retreat, once I was sure she couldn't come after me, and here you are, standing in my way."

"You didn't have to bite me. You could have gone around me."

"I saw you as a threat. Someone who would tell on me. Someone who would kill me if you could have."

"I could have," Letta said. "Believe me, I could have."

Hannah sobered a bit with the news. "Sorry."

Letta didn't feel that the wolf shifter's word was sincere. If Letta was in charge here, she'd leave Hannah in that cage for a very long time, until she learned to apologize and mean it. "You bit Bryan, a human friend of your own?"

Hannah glanced at the cages where Mark and Bryan were watching her, neither of them shifting out of their wolf forms. Letta thought they might not be able to. She felt bad for them because they hadn't done anything to deserve this. Well, neither had she!

"Sorry, Bryan. You tried to stop me, and I couldn't allow it. I was…kind out of my head when I turned into a wolf and I was frightened. Ena already hated my guts, and I figured that would be the last straw."

Letta really liked Ena, and she couldn't imagine the dragon fae shifter would treat anyone poorly without good reason. "So why don't you and Ena get along?"

Hannah shrugged.

Letta glanced at the wolves. They would know the truth, if they could shift and tell her. But neither was shifting.

Simon suddenly entered the hut with a collar in hand, and his gaze drifted from her to Hannah.

Letta closed her gaping mouth. He was going to put a restraining collar on her so she couldn't run off? She so wished she had woken last night and slipped out of there when she could have.

"So you can shift on your own now?" he asked Hannah, pausing at Letta's cage door.

"Yeah." Hannah shifted three times for him to prove it.

"Good." Then he turned to Letta. "Don't give me any trouble, and you can come join Myla and me for breakfast."

Letta would like to have breakfast with Myla, but she didn't want to have anything to do with Simon.

He unlocked the cage door. "You're doing great so far."

It appeared he wasn't letting Hannah out of her cage anytime soon, and, since she wouldn't apologize with any real conviction to Letta, she hoped she stayed in there for a lot longer.

Letta nodded, and he opened the cage door. He still approached her with caution, with a wolf's wariness. But she wasn't going to do anything to jeopardize her freedom for even a few precious moments. The more they let her out and she showed she could be trusted, the better chance she had of running off.

He put the collar on her neck, his fingers touching her skin and she felt some kind of strange kinship, as a wolf, she guessed, but more too, as if this darkly, annoying wolf was fascinated with her. As much as she loathed to admit it to herself, she felt just as much fascination for him.

Either she'd gone mad, or this was all so new to her, that she couldn't control how she was feeling.

He pulled his hands away from her neck and motioned for her to lead.

The iron collar would keep her from fae transporting out of here, but couldn't she just shift into the wolf and run off? She suspected there was more to the collar than met the eye.

"I could let you learn the truth on your own. Sometimes experience is better than being warned about something." He walked her through the woods to another hut.

She knew it.

"We have adapted the collar to be like one that a human uses to control his dog."

She frowned, not following what he was saying.

"It zaps the dog into compliance when a trigger mechanism is used. It makes for an obedient wolf when one is being obstinate."

She wanted to shift and bite him right then and there.

He smiled knowingly at her. He must have smelled her scent change from annoyed to aggressive. She wasn't used to being able to use her sense of smell to detect changes in a person's emotions. It could come in handy, once she was more aware of it. She wondered if there was any way of controlling her own scent, so she wouldn't be an open book for other shifters who would be well-aware of what she was feeling.

They entered the hut and she smelled both Myla and Simon's scent the strongest. She wondered if they lived in the cottage together. Myla was looking so much better, Letta smiled at her.

"I'm fixing eggs and bacon. Thanks again for all your care. Simon tells me you have your shifting under control." Myla motioned to a chair, indicating she wanted Letta to sit there.

Letta asked instead, "Can I help you without anything? You look really well today, so much better than yesterday."

"Thank you, no. I'm just serving up the food. And you look good too."

"I'm feeling much better, thanks."

Simon took a seat across from them. "The humans haven't changed from wolf to human again."

"Fae, right?" Letta asked. They weren't humans any longer.

"Right."

Myla smiled at Letta and served up the food.

"But Hannah demonstrated she can shift. She says

78

you attacked her first," Simon said.

"She's right." Myla served up the food and coffee. "I was protecting the treasure, as was my job. The wolf was unknown to me. I only growled, raised my hackles, and meant to chase her off. She acted like she didn't understand the cues I was giving off. I raced at her to snap at her, not intending to bite her unless she still didn't leave, and she attacked me. I'm sure to her, it looked like I was attacking her. And once we knew she had only come into her wolf shifter abilities, we also know that she probably didn't have much control over her behavior and didn't know how to react."

"She's alpha." Letta took a bite of her eggs. "These are great."

"Thanks. Yeah, she's alpha." Myla added sugar and cream to her coffee.

"Ena doesn't like her, that much is sure," Simon said.

"Do you think Hannah's made a play for her mate?" Letta asked.

Simon smiled at her, and Letta felt her cheeks fill with heat. Then he finished off his eggs. "You'll watch over Letta while I'm gone?"

Letta couldn't believe he'd leave her in the custody of his sister. Then again, her sister was a wolf, a guard wolf, and she would most likely do her duty and keep Letta in line.

"Yeah, sure. Go do whatever you have to do. What about the others?" Myla asked.

"They stay in their cages. They need to be fed, but

they won't be released. I don't trust Hannah. As to the men, I don't trust them either, but only because they're so new to all of this. Hannah? I imagine she's going to give us trouble." Then he looked at Letta.

She wondered just what he thought about her.

Simon finished his coffee. "Letta can stay with us tonight at the cottage, if all goes well today."

Myla smiled. Letta didn't. Did he mean that she would be stuck living with him in the same cottage? Ugh.

Simon smiled at Letta, as if he knew just what she was thinking. "I'll be back as soon as I can." Then he left, and Letta finished her breakfast.

"He's all right." Myla started clearing away the dishes. "He's just ultra-protective of me."

Letta helped her clean the dishes. "Were you sleeping with me as a wolf last night for a long time?"

"Yeah, you are kind of like a new wolf pup, needing a pack mate to give you comfort. You hadn't hurt anyone, and from the way you reacted to me, your actions indicated you wouldn't hurt me either. I stayed for half the night, then Simon made our healer and me leave to get some rest. I wouldn't have agreed to it unless he stayed with you to keep you company in case you woke."

"He stayed all night."

Myla smiled. Someone knocked on the door of the cottage, and Myla got up and glanced out the window and frowned. "Oh no, I should have warned you. Gia is here and she's a wolf who has the hots for Simon."

"So?" Like that meant anything to Letta.

"Gia is afraid you will try to steal him away."

"She doesn't have to worry about me in that regard."

"Gia didn't like that you and Simon slept together in the cage all night."

"As if that was my choice! And he was across the cage from me, not sleeping with me."

Myla chuckled and opened the door. "Hi, Gia. Do you want to come in for some coffee?"

"Sure." Gia entered the cottage, her red hair twisted into a bun in back, her green eyes narrowed as she gave Letta the once-over in a way that said she'd like to rip her throat out as a wolf if she could.

Letta carried the fresh mugs of coffee to the table. She couldn't believe the wolf would be worried about her wanting any intimacy between her and Simon.

"So what are you going to do with her?" Gia asked Myla, then turned her attention to Letta, her look malevolent.

"Simon wants to keep her in the pack. She's a healer, and she has some…special skills."

Gia turned her attention again to Myla. "Such as?"

"Special…*combat* skills. Magical skills. I wouldn't want to test her." Myla almost looked happy to share that bit of news with Gia.

Letta was afraid Gia would try to provoke her just to see what she could do. Maybe even discredit her as being a viable member of the pack, if she forced Letta to fight her. Which was fine by her. She still had Ena's offer to be her midwife, and she had every intention of taking her up on it.

"You fed her. You've done your duty. Do you want me to take her back to her cage?" Gia smiled a little evilly at the prospect.

"She's not going back there. She proved to Simon she can control her shifting and she did save my life," Myla said.

Gia's smile slipped. "Yet he put a *collar* on her."

"Yes, so she'll stay with us and we can teach her our ways."

"It sounds to me like he doesn't trust her." Gia eyed the collar.

Letta had hope then. The woman hated her, and Letta thought she might want to remove the collar from around Letta's neck so she could leave. Then Gia would be free to have Simon like she wanted.

Letta just had to figure out a way to see Gia on her own, without anyone stopping them, if Gia was even agreeable. Gia might realize it could backfire and Simon would be furious with her.

Maybe Letta could tell her that she could pretend to threaten her with her magic, and Gia removed the collar out of fear. Letta smiled. That's just what she'd do as soon as she could meet up with her privately.

CHAPTER 7

Simon soon met up with Princess Alicia at her castle, but he wasn't surprised to see Ena there to speak with her also. Good. He could question Ena about Hannah and give her a report about how Myla and Letta were doing. The news about the two men and Hannah wasn't as promising.

"What are you doing here?" Ena sounded irritated that Simon was there.

Princess Alicia smiled. "Why don't we go into my sitting room and talk over whatever you came to see me concerning."

Alicia led the way and then they all took their seats on blue velvet couches covered in gold embroidery. Simon bit his tongue before he questioned Alicia, allowing Ena to go first. Ena was a princess too now, and she'd also saved Alicia's life, so they had a special bond. *He* could be considered the king of his wolf back, though they didn't have titles like that. He was the leader of his pack and that was good enough for him.

"Ena?"

"I suspect Simon and I are here for the same reason. A fae showed up in his territory and she saved Myla's life after—"

"Wait, Halloran told me about all this last night. How is Myla doing?" Alicia asked Ena.

Ena deferred to Simon to answer the question.

"She's much better," Simon said. "Thanks for asking. She is up and about and feeling like her old self."

"What about Letta, Bryan, and Mark?" Ena asked, now that they were on the subject of the wounded and newly-turned wolves.

"Letta seems to have good control over her wolf shifting. Myla slept with her half the night. I slept with them both and when Myla left, I continued to stay with the woman."

Ena's brows rose.

"I mean, as her guard."

"So she was turned also," Ena said, frowning.

"Right. As to Mark and Bryan, they were wolves this morning. They seem to have no control over their shifting. They're still in their cages and being well-cared for. Letta is staying with Myla and me in our cottage."

Ena raised a brow in speculation.

"I wouldn't put her up with anyone else while we know so little about her." He frowned at the annoying dragon fae shifter.

"Good. Now, Halloran said the woman who saved Myla's life is Letta. For your information, she's one of the scorpion fae. And yes, she was telling the truth when she said she had met us before," Alicia said.

Both Simon and Ena closed their gaping mouths. Simon spoke first after that. "They no longer exist. The race died off centuries ago."

"They didn't though. They took us hostage, fed us, and released us. We had no idea where we were when this all happened. Their king looked like a boy, but it was fae glamor. They were so warlike, they practically annihilated their kind, you're right. But when each of their kind come of age, they move on and live among other fae."

Simon didn't like the idea of that one bit. "So she's not a woodland fae, but a scorpion fae." Her fae aura was silvery when he'd first seen her, but after the wolf changed her, now it was more of a silvery green.

"She's a wolf fae shifter now," Alicia said. "And she's your charge."

He didn't need to be told that.

"Unless he's afraid to keep her in their village, and she'll come home with me." Ena folded her arms.

"She stays with me. With my people." Why did he sound like he wanted to keep the woman for himself when she could be real trouble for their kind? For any fae kind? "I have a question for you though, Ena. What is the matter with Hannah that you and she don't seem to get along?"

"Has she been pleasant to you?" Ena asked.

"I think she was making the attempt when she thought it could free her from the cage."

"Was she able to control her shifting?"

"Yes. She only showed me she could when she thought it would benefit her though," he said.

Ena shook her head. "She is contrary and won't work unless her life depends on it. She was supposed to be working with Mark and Bryan on the gardens, but she did as little as possible. Before she came to our world, she was the leader of a group of fae seers who were trying to kill our kind. Bryan and Mark tried to convince her to do her fair share of work in the gardens, but I know they were covering for her. Whenever I returned to the castle after a flight somewhere, I'd swoop over the gardens to see what she was doing. Bryan and Mark would be busy weeding or planting new plants. Hannah? Sitting on her butt on a bench watching, as if she was too good to dirty her hands. When we had rescued him from the fae seers, Bryan wanted to take her with us, thinking she could be a fae like us, given time. And he knew any fae seers would kill her if she had been living there still. You may keep her. I don't want her back. She is one of you anyway. Maybe you can work with her and she will come around."

"But you doubt it." Simon could tell from Ena's whole expression that she thought the woman was nothing but trouble.

Ena shrugged. "I doubt she would behave for me.

Maybe, since you're a wolf, and she's one also now, you'll have better luck with her."

"All right, thanks, princess. Princess." Simon got up to leave.

"Thanks for the update," Alicia said. "My mother wondered if Mark will be able to plan her gardens anytime soon. She realized he might not be able to."

"It remains to be seen. But if they get their shifting under control, we'll send him or Bryan back to her." Simon then left the sitting room, glad for answers, but worried about Letta's scorpion fae heritage. He suspected Hannah was going to be way more trouble than she was worth. Hopefully, like Ena said, the wolves might be able to get her under control.

Before Simon could get very far down the hall, Ena chased after him, surprising him. "Wait! I'm sorry if I've been kind of out of sorts with you—"

Simon took hold of Ena's arm in a comforting way. "Our women get that way when they are having little ones. I fully understand." Though it had taken him a while to realize that was the issue and the healer had confirmed that could be the reason.

"Thank you. And if you don't need Letta around and think she's safe to be with us and she still wants to come live with us, we'd be happy to take her in."

He bowed his head to Ena, and then he left the castle, then fae traveled home. He wouldn't wish Letta on any other fae, if she was as warlike as her predecessors. Not when she was now a wolf too. He wondered if they didn't have an immunity to the wolf shifter's bite then because they were such an ancient race.

He was rethinking the notion of letting her roam freely. They might have her collared so she couldn't leave, but she could still use her magic to hurt his people. That worried him where Myla was concerned. Yet, the two of them seemed to enjoy each other's company. He probably had nothing to worry about with regard to Myla and her. Still, what if Letta just…snapped?

When he finally reached his and Myla's cottage, he smelled Gia's scent. Now *she* could be real trouble, and he hadn't even considered how much so with so much else up in the air. He knew she was interested in him, trying to capture his attention, trying to help out when he didn't need her help. She probably had learned he was guarding Letta last night and didn't like it.

He opened the door to the cottage and all the women turned to look at him. "Gia?"

She smiled brightly at him. She was a pretty brunette and she was a good fighter, but he just didn't feel any attraction to her.

"I need to speak with my sister and Letta in private."

Gia's face fell. She sliced a glower at Letta, which concerned him. Then she managed a small smile for Simon, inclined her head, and hurried out of the cottage.

Simon shut the door and Myla looked concerned that he didn't have good news. Which he didn't. "Letta is a scorpion fae."

Myla turned her head sharply to look at Letta.

Letta stood and appeared resigned to her fate. "Did you want to take me back to the cage or release me so I can find another place to live?"

Simon frowned at her. "Are you going to cause us trouble?"

"Why would I do that?" she asked Simon, sounding annoyed.

"The scorpion fae destroyed their own kind."

"Many did. I wasn't raised by those who had killed the others. I give you my word I don't plan to take over your wolf pack or kill any of your people, unless it's in my own self-defense."

He couldn't believe she was now saying she was willing to stay with them. "You've had a change of heart about staying with us?" He suspected she thought he'd remove her collar if he believed she wouldn't run away.

"I was born a healer. That's my inherent talent." She didn't answer him about staying with them.

"And the magic you used to repel the brown wolf?"

"A defensive mechanism."

"That you could use in an offensive manner," Simon said.

"I could, but I don't. I have no reason to. Not unless I'm attacked. And then it would only be to protect myself. None of our kind are supposed to tell others what we truly are. We made up the woodland fae name to disguise the fact that we are the offspring of the scorpion fae. But the fae who fought each other died. I don't know why our king told Princess Alicia and the others who we were.

Maybe as a warning, because he knows that much fighting continues to go on between the fae kingdoms. In any event, none of the rest of us have ever been involved in a war. Once we're of mating age, we have to seek our way in the world. That's all," Letta said. "I know you don't trust me, and I can only show you that you have nothing to fear from me. Hannah is another story. She showed no remorse for biting me or the others."

Simon nodded. "We will see how she reacts to Myla then. You can stay here and make yourself comfortable, Letta. Myla, come with me to see Hannah and tell me what you think about her. She seems to be shifting all right, but I don't want to release her yet if she could continue to be a problem to you or anyone else in the pack after what she did to you, Bryan, and Letta."

"Can I wander around the grounds?" Letta asked.

"You can. Just a cautionary note, your collar will tingle before it zaps you, if you get beyond a safe distance from the village. If you get even farther out from the village, it'll knock you out."

"Good to know." Letta didn't sound like she was worried, concerning the prospect, which made him wonder what she might be up to.

She went outside with them, and then took a path away from the hut where the wolves were caged.

Simon suspected she was going to check out the layout of the village and learn the best way to escape when she had her chance. He saw Gia watching the situation and he gave her a look that told her to leave

Letta alone. He was afraid she'd give the scorpion fae a hard time, and who knew where that might lead.

"What did you want to talk to me about? In private?" Myla asked Simon.

"Do you think it's going to be safe with her here?" He watched as Letta disappeared into the woods, the village comprised of cottages located throughout the woods, not like a human village where the trees would surround the village. The wolves liked their woods.

"Letta?" his sister asked.

"Yes."

"I think she's going to be fine unless Gia gives her grief."

He let out his breath in annoyance. "I don't know why the woman can't get the message that I'm not interested in mating her. Gia won't become my pack leader mate. She rubs too many of our pack members the wrong way. Particularly the she-wolves. She only makes an effort with you because you're my sister and she knows I'd be all over her case if she gave you trouble."

Myla smiled. "I really like Letta. She and I just hit it off great. Like we've been friends forever. You know how it is when you just bond right away with someone. Hannah is a different story. I'd just as soon send her on her way. Oh, and why did you fit Letta with a non-punishing collar? If you're worried she might try to leave?"

"I didn't want to hurt her. I just wanted to pretend she could be hurt so that she won't try and leave."

"If she's doing okay with her shifting, why not let her leave?"

"She still needs to learn our ways, for her protection."

"Nothing more?" Myla smiled at him. "We've been wolves since birth. I know when you're interested in a she-wolf. Most you've shown any interest in have come and gone, but that was when you were younger, and you weren't leading the pack. This one's different."

"This one's a scorpion fae."

"Well, there is that. Maybe that's what intrigues you about her. She's unique. Brett was closer to her when she fainted, and yet there you were, jumping in to rescue her before she hit the floor. Everyone there who observed your actions knew, like I do, that there's something more going on between the two of you. And then you slept with her all night."

"*Guarding* her."

Myla chuckled. "Right. As if she needed a guard. And if she had, you could have assigned someone the job and he would have stayed on the outside of the cage."

"I had to make sure she didn't grow ill again."

"Right. She likes you too, Simon," Myla said.

Simon snorted. "She's looking for a way to get out of here as fast as she can."

"And whose fault is that?" Myla glanced at him as they stood in the woods near the path that would lead them to the hut housing the caged wolves.

"Your safety was what was most important."

"All right, but if you really want her to stay, and not because you believe she belongs with the pack, solely because she's a wolf and she needs to learn our ways, then let her know it. You're the pack leader. You're the one who will have the most influence over her."

"She is determined to join Ena and the dragon fae."

"She will be happy to live with her own kind, once she sees we all accept her. She has done nothing to indicate she would be a danger to any of us."

They entered the hut where the cages were and found the men were now in their human forms.

"Did you eat?" Myla asked them.

"Yes. As soon as we left our wolf coats behind," Mark said. "When can we leave the cages?"

"When you have complete control over your shifting," Simon said. "Can you turn into wolves? Either of you?"

Mark shook his head. "I was just finally able to shift so I could eat like a human."

"You're fae now, no longer human. You're wolf shifter fae," Simon said. "Try and turn into a wolf for me."

Bryan groaned. "It's like Mark said. We finally were able to shift back to our...uhm, fae form."

"Simon is right. The faster you get control of your shifting, the sooner you can leave the cages and you can live with someone in one of the cottages," Myla said. "Besides, if you controlled the shift so that you could eat in your fae form, there's hope you can do it again."

Both Mark and Bryan wrinkled their foreheads as they concentrated, and Bryan shifted.

"Woah," Mark said, "good going, Bryan."

"He's been a wolf longer than you have, Mark, so it might take a little longer for you to get the hang of it," Simon said. "Keep trying though. And, Bryan, shift back."

Bryan shifted back and pumped his fist in victory. "You can do it, Mark, just keep trying."

But Mark couldn't. Still, Bryan practiced shifting back and forth and looked thrilled to be getting used to it.

"We'll leave you here for another day so you can keep Mark company and encourage him," Simon said, "but if you can prove you're doing well with shifting, and you're not going to bite anyone—though I'll tell you right now if you do, you'll be in for a fight—we can release you. We'll have someone fix you with collars so you can leave for exercise and other business."

Then Myla looked at an obstinate Hannah sitting on her mat, watching the guys, and then Simon and Myla.

"So you're shifting all right now," Myla said to her.

"Yep. Fancy that."

"And you killed fae when you were a human," Myla said.

Hannah didn't say anything to that.

"You could apologize for the wounds you gave Myla," Simon said.

"What about the wounds she gave me!" Hannah

said, her tone belligerent.

"It appears yours didn't last long."

Hannah folded her arms. "Hers are healed too."

Simon frowned at her. "Apologize to Myla for injuring her so badly."

Hannah chewed on her bottom lip, then said, "Sorry, Myla. But if you hadn't attacked first, none of this would have happened." She smiled.

Myla smiled at her, but Simon knew that look. If he agreed, Myla would keep the wolf caged up for the rest of her life. He didn't blame his sister in the least. He would leave Hannah in the cage for a little while longer too.

When Simon and his sister left the hut, he intended to locate Letta, when they saw her with one of his bachelor brothers, and Aegis looked way too interested in Letta.

"Well, you might not have to convince her to stay if another wolf, even one of our brothers, can encourage her to join us permanently," Myla said. "I'm heading home, so you can attend to whatever needs attending to, regarding leading the pack."

"I'll be back for the noon meal."

"See you then." Myla headed home and Simon stalked toward Aegis and Letta.

Letta was nodding as Aegis talked to her, animatedly motioning with his hands, smiling, definitely interested in the woman and Simon had to put a stop to it. He reasoned that Letta still could prove to be dangerous to their kind and he didn't want her to hurt any of his people. Besides, his brother had work to do.

"Aegis," Simon snapped to get his attention, frowning at his brother. "Don't you have guard duty for Alton's treasure right about now?"

"It's Myla's turn. Uh, oh, yeah. Sorry, Simon. I forgot I was taking her place until she's completely healed." Aegis smiled broadly at Letta. "I'll see you later." Then he hurried off.

Letta frowned at Simon, then walked off. He hurried to join her.

"You want me to stay with your pack, right?" Letta asked.

"Of course."

"Then I'll find a wolf to mate. When I was with the others of my kind, we weren't allowed to have boyfriends. That's one of the reasons I left."

Simon didn't think she was being serious. She just got here. He knew she was annoyed with him for interrupting her visit with Aegis.

"Or is it that you object to Aegis for some other reason?"

"My brother is a good man, but he had agreed to take Myla's guard duty. Even though she's healed well, she can't stay in the cold, damp cave or fight, if she has to, until we know she's fully recovered."

"I understand. So are you releasing Hannah soon?"

"No. I don't trust the wolf."

"That makes two of us. Though you don't even trust

me."

"She's injured people. You're capable of it but haven't used your powers to hurt anyone yet, except for protecting yourself against Hannah's attack. And you didn't leave any permanent injury."

Letta sighed. "True. Did you know Gia doesn't like me."

Simon didn't say anything. He was afraid Letta was coming up with a reason to excuse a future fight between her and Gia.

Letta glanced at Simon. "So what do I do about it?"

"What do you do about what?" Simon wondered if it was a good idea to have Letta staying with him and his sister. Yet, the reason he was doing so was to protect his people from her should she become combative.

"Gia's not liking me? If I mated another wolf, she'd know I wasn't interested in becoming your mate."

"She knows you're not interested in me."

"That's not what she said. She's furious that you slept with me."

Simon pulled Letta to a stop, his face feeling flushed all at once. "I did *not* sleep with you."

"But you really did. All night long too. Not the way she thinks, maybe, but you were there with me. Anyway, I might have only just become a wolf, but I've always had good instincts where people's emotions are concerned, even if they're trying to hide them from me."

He felt his face flush again.

"I know when someone likes or dislikes me. And she

97

very much dislikes me. When she comes to fight me, what do I do? Let her tear into me? Take the injures to prove I'm not a warrior fae at heart? Or fight her to show I won't be intimidated by the likes of her? What would two wolves of your pack do who can't come to an agreement with each other and tempers flare?"

"You keep the peace and I'll take her to task."

"Is that what wolves in your pack would do? I thought they'd deal with it on their own."

"Sometimes our males get a little aggressive over a female or for other reasons and they snarl, and growl, and bite."

"Teach me how to do this."

"What?" He frowned at her. He didn't want to teach her how to fight and hurt another wolf.

"I don't know how to take care of myself in a wolf fight. If you want me to protect myself, I'll have to learn how."

"Not by me."

"Of course not. You're the leader. Your people might think I'm trying to take over."

He gave her a smug smile. As if she could do that. "I'm a male."

"You sure are."

Simon shook his head. "You would need to fight a she-wolf. Practice fight."

"Myla?"

"When she's all healed up, I'm sure she'll love to teach you."

"I'd fight Hannah, but I wouldn't play-fight."

"Holding a bit of a grudge, are we?"

"Yeah. She had no reason to bite me."

"We're getting too far out. Your collar will begin to let you know that you are. Let's go back. Myla's returned to the house if you want to visit with her further." Simon hadn't realized just how far away from the village they'd walked, and he didn't want Letta to know her collar would do nothing but prevent her from fae travelling. Though he could give her a jolt if she tried to kill one of their wolves with the controller he had in his pouch. But for her collar to just go off when she went too far out from the village? It wouldn't happen and he didn't want her to learn what he told her wasn't true.

CHAPTER 8

While Letta and Simon made their way back through the woods, she was actually rethinking leaving the Wolf Mountain territory, now that she had become a wolf shifter. Even though the wolves weren't her people, she was now more like them than her own people. Being a scorpion fae among the dragon fae wasn't the same as being a wolf shifter among them.

So why not join the wolf pack? Hopefully, she wouldn't have to kill Gia. No way was she letting Simon fight her battles for her. She figured, even if she didn't know all the nuances of fighting, she would still have some instinctive sense about it if Gia decided to attack. At least Letta hoped so.

She also thought she needed to learn how to fight male wolves, just to get in practice with a much heftier wolf. That might help her against a really aggressive female. She was certain Myla would be too gentle with

Letta, worried she'd injure her.

Then Letta smiled. She could ask Simon's brother, Aegis, to play-fight with her. He might be willing.

Hannah wouldn't be her friend, she was sure. But she'd met several other wolves in the pack who had thanked her for saving Myla's life and seemed genuinely interested in welcoming her to the pack. She'd even met Simon and Myla's sister, Kirsten, and her four wolf cubs. Kirsten had warned Letta not to let Simon boss her around too much, which Letta appreciated.

She wondered about the collar and if it wasn't working. She hadn't realized she and Simon had walked so far out of the village, until they began walking back and it took them forever to begin seeing cottages in the woods again. She hadn't really been testing the collar, just wanting to really meet everyone she could and see the layout of the place.

"How are Mark and Bryan doing?" she finally asked Simon as they both had been really quiet, and she wondered what Simon had been thinking about.

"Bryan has had more time to be one of us and he's doing well with his shifting. Mark couldn't shift on command. As soon as they have more control over it, they will reside with a couple of my bachelor brothers."

"And they will teach them how to fight?"

"It's not all about fighting, but playing, showing who's in charge, finding food, and learning how to use our enhanced senses. For them, it's not just about being new wolf-shifters, but about—"

"Being fae. Fae travel, and everything else they'll need to learn about as fae. When they return to the human world, they'll have an aura that fae-seers will be able to see, so it will be much more dangerous for them."

"Exactly. They are one of us now, and that will take some time for them to get used to. Though they've been here for a couple of years now, living among the fae, helping the dragon shifters with their battles, and working hard for their keep. We would welcome them to continue to live among the wolf shifter fae."

"When will they be able to return to Ena and Brett's castle?"

"They may never return. Not if they find they like it here well enough, living among their own kind. They might even find mates among the females in the pack."

"Couldn't they take their mates with them?" Letta wondered then if Simon worried about losing a couple of his wolves, should Mark and Bryan fall for she-wolves in his pack and leave.

"I think we're getting ahead of ourselves."

Just then they saw the shadows of two dragons flying overhead, and they looked up to see Ena and Brett flying over the village.

"They're returning?"

"Ena better not think she's taking you home with her."

But the dragons flew beyond the village.

She and Simon reached his cottage, and she thanked him for the escort, then they saw Brett and Ena flying back overhead. This time, Brett had a goat in his talons.

"What are they doing with the goat?" she asked, horrified, thinking the dragons planned to eat it.

"From what I understand, the goat went missing. The dragons find objects, missing animals, people, and have any number of other kinds of missions, some taking them to the human world. Their jobs can be dangerous. In this case, it appears they've found someone's lost goat."

Now she wished she could be a dragon too. She liked the idea of helping others out like they did. Maybe she could go with them on their missions as a healer, if they needed her help. "That's why they have all the treasure. They're paid for their services with it."

"That's correct." Simon bowed his head to her. "I'll see you at the noon meal."

She inclined her head and went inside, but she wasn't done exploring. Myla was lying on a couch, sleeping. Letta went over to her, but as soon as she moved, Myla's eyes opened. "Oh, Letta, I hope you enjoyed your jaunt around the village."

"I did. I was walking with Simon. Are you ill? Feverish?" Letta placed her hand on Myla's forehead.

"No, thanks, Letta. Just tired."

"You *were* injured badly."

"Yeah, but I'm getting better. I think I just overdid it."

"What can I do for you?"

"Nothing, really. You can help me make the noon

meal later, if you'd like."

"I'll do that. I haven't finished exploring the village. If you don't need me or the healer…"

"No, go on. Enjoy yourself."

Letta didn't want to disturb Myla while she tried to sleep if she remained in the cottage. She slipped outside and decided to roam around in her wolf coat. She really wanted to remove the retaining collar too, to show Simon he couldn't control her like he thought he could. If she stayed, it was because she wanted to. She ran through the woods in a different direction this time, racing off as far as she could go, loving the way her wolf legs propelled her so much faster than her fae legs. She ran until she realized she had to be way beyond the boundaries of the wolf village and not once had her collar tingled to warn her it was going to give her a shock. Had Simon lied to her?

She would have been irritated with him, except that she appreciated that he hadn't really attached a collar that would shock her.

She kept going farther and farther away, heading in the direction of the dragon territory. If she could, she'd find Ena and see if she could have someone remove her collar. Then she'd transport back to the wolf village, hopefully in time to help Myla fix lunch, and prove to Simon she was safe to be around, and she wouldn't be under his control any longer.

The problem was she couldn't see Ena's fae dust trail because she and Brett had been flying as dragons. Letta kept going, hoping she'd smell dragon scents, even Alton's, though she suspected he still wasn't happy with her learning his treasure was in the cave in Wolf Mountain territory. Now that she was a wolf, though, maybe he'd believe she would want to help guard his treasure. She would have to earn her keep while living with the wolf pack.

As far as she'd run, stopping to drink at a creek, and taking off again, she was way beyond where the collar should have worked. She smiled a little. So Simon hadn't been so bad after all. If he could try to make her mind with the collar though, as if he had some kind of control to operate it, she was probably beyond his reach now.

Then she thought she heard something following her through the brush and she turned to look, but she saw nothing. Still, as she continued to move forward, she kept hearing sounds of movement through the brush behind her. Another wolf? Or something else? She'd encountered one wild boar out in the woods when she first had come to the region, and she had managed to climb a tree before he gored her.

She couldn't climb a tree as a wolf though. She shifted and stopped. The creature, whatever it was, stopped too. Simon? Following her to see where she'd go? But she didn't think he'd wait. He'd approach her and give her grief for leaving the village.

Then a tan-colored wolf with a black saddle of fur on her back lunged out of the woods at her and Letta quickly shifted, thinking maybe she should have used her scorpion fae magic instead. The wolf appeared to be in killing form, not intending to return her to the village. The wolf plowed into Letta and knocked her down. Letta smelled her scent. It was *Gia. Not* surprising.

This was not the time to show any weakness, Letta told herself, and scrambled to her feet.

But the wolf attacked again, snarling, biting, and growling. If Gia managed to kill Letta, she thought the wolf would tell Simon she tried to convince her to return, but Letta attacked her, and she couldn't do anything but fight back.

Letta wasn't going to let Gia win. Right then and there, Letta decided she was going to win Simon's affection, if she could keep from killing the wolf and stay alive at the same time. If she could have fae transported out of there, she would have. That had been the only thing about the collar that Simon had said that was the truth. She tried to leave and couldn't. If she didn't win against the wolf, he could have signed Letta's death warrant.

Would he care, or would he figure it served her right for running off? And would he believe the lies Letta was sure Gia would tell him when she returned to the village?

Letta growled right back and attacked the wolf, her scorpion-warrior aggressiveness coming to the forefront. No one tried to kill her kind without paying the consequences. Even so, Letta knew she was at a strong disadvantage since she had never fought as a wolf before. The wolf had already torn at Letta's shoulder, though

Letta wasn't feeling the pain kick in yet, due to the adrenaline flooding her bloodstream. She smelled her blood though, and that outraged Letta even more. She tore into Gia, not wanting to prove to Simon she was as dangerous as he thought her kind were, but she wasn't going to let the wolf get away with this.

Letta had torn into Gia's flank, her neck, her cheek. She knew she needed to go for the throat, but she was trying too hard to keep Gia from grabbing hers and killing her. Then she had the brilliant notion of going for one of Gia's legs. The problem with that was that if she attacked low and didn't manage to bite the wolf's leg and break it before Gia bit her spine, Letta would be a dead wolf.

And Letta was wearing out. Gia was about the same size as her, but the wolf was good at feints, and dodging her, making Letta waste a lot of energy and not getting anything accomplished, wearing her down. Then Gia was getting in a lot more bites too, and Letta was sure her blood loss was weakening her also.

Then Letta thought of a good way to take care of Gia without getting herself into much more trouble. Though she knew when she tried it, she might give Gia the chance to make the killing blow.

Still, Letta knew now, she couldn't get the advantage without some help. She quickly lifted her chin and howled, calling for anyone in the vicinity to aid her. Maybe one of the dragons would be near and could swoop down and carry her away.

Gia had come in for the charge, but then she suddenly stopped, as if she knew she was going to be in really big trouble now. Then again, it would only be Letta's word against hers, and if Letta was dead, Gia would have the sole chance to tell the story.

Gia growled at her, trying to figure out what she wanted to do next, Letta suspected.

Letta was gasping for breath, trying to get ready for the next battle exchange. When Gia didn't come in to fight her, Letta howled again, afraid no one was going to hear her, or know what she needed.

Gia took the opportunity to attack. Maybe that's what she was waiting for. Letta to make herself more vulnerable so she couldn't hurt Gia any further. It didn't work. Letta jumped away, and Gia bit her in the rump. Letta yelped like a scared pup, and rounded on the wolf, their paws resting on each shoulders, dancing on their hind legs, biting each other's mouth when Letta knew she couldn't last, her bites and growls not as powerful, her legs weakening.

She tried to bolt away and Gia fell on her like a rabid wolf, ready to kill her. Letta shifted, knowing it was a dangerous thing to do, a fae no match for a wolf's teeth, but she had to try and use her own magic to save herself. She rolled to give her time to cast her electrical charge, the wolf missing her throat and clamping down on her shoulder again. Letta heard movement, lots of movement, but the wolf wasn't giving up and Letta had no choice. Die, or use her magic. She zapped the wolf hard, not enough to kill her, not yet, but it knocked Gia off her. Gia sat stunned for a moment as wolves filled the woods.

Letta could barely look up to see Simon leading a pack of males, but even Myla was with them, and she felt so bad that Myla had come looking for her when she hadn't fully recovered herself yet. That's the last Letta remembered, her final thought: she needed to live to tell her story, whether anyone believed her or not—everything fading to black after that.

CHAPTER 9

Simon knew he was going to have real trouble now. The problem wasn't just Gia, but her three brothers. They could be real hotheads and when they saw what Letta had done to Gia, ignoring what the wolf had done to the scorpion-wolf, he knew he was in for a fight. He also knew just whose fault this was. Well, Letta's for running off, but he knew Gia was the one who chased her down and tried to kill her.

He really couldn't blame Letta for making a run for it either. Wolves didn't like to be incarcerated, free-spirits that they were. Well, truth be told, none of the fae did. But she would have been safe if she'd stayed with them. Gia wouldn't have dared to hurt Letta in the village, and even if she had attacked her, it would never have gotten this far.

He hadn't wanted Myla to go with them, but as soon as she learned Letta was missing, she thought she could convince her to come back to the pack. When they smelled Gia's scent all along the trail that Letta had left, they knew the wolf was after her, and that she hadn't intended to bring her back to the village either.

At some point, Gia's brothers had joined up with them. Simon had regretted that, until he thought that it was better that they see the situation for themselves, whatever it was, than letting the other wolves there explain what they had seen.

He and Myla stripped some fabric off their clothes to make the bandages, then wrapped them around Letta's wounds the best they could. Gia's brothers had done the same for her, but she wasn't as bad off.

Carrying Letta in his arms, to show the other wolves with him that he was her protector—and nobody better find fault with her over fighting Gia—Simon headed home.

Letta was unconscious; Gia was wide awake, and her brother Tomas was carrying her back to the village.

"She goes now," Tomas said to Simon.

"Gia?" Simon glowered at Tomas, who was wearing his own stormy expression.

No wolf told Simon what to do with regard to the wolves of his pack. And for now, Letta was a wolf in their pack, until he said otherwise.

"She's a danger to our females," Tomas growled.

"Gia is. Yes."

Myla was trying to keep up with Simon and he wanted to slow down for her, worried she wasn't feeling well still, surprised she'd been sleeping when he'd returned home to check on what she and Letta had been doing. But *he* couldn't slow down, not when he was so concerned about Letta's wounds. She needed to see the healer at once. If she didn't make it, he was banishing Gia from the pack. Her brothers too, if they couldn't live with his decision. That was a strict possibility anyway, even if Letta recovered. He wouldn't allow for anarchy in his pack. What Gia did was wrong and went against everything he stood for.

Letta stirred in his arms and muttered, "Bad wolf." But that's all she said and then she seemed to be somewhere else far from here.

He hated the idea that if he'd let her go to live with Ena and Brett, none of this would ever have happened.

"I know what you're thinking, brother," Myla said, sounding way out of breath, "but you can't think in that way."

Myla couldn't read minds, but she got darn close to reading his. "Myla, slow down and walk with some of the other men. Or someone's going to have to carry you back too."

She snorted, but she did slow her pace and their brother Ronan stayed with her to carry her back home if he needed to.

The women had run a long way and it took them forever to reach the village. Now he had a problem. They had one healer, and two injured wolves. Since he knew Letta wasn't the one at fault and she was injured worse, he wanted her seen to first. But he knew there were already hard feelings that she and Gia had battled each other. Simon suspected Gia's brothers believed that if Letta hadn't come into the pack, Gia would have been his choice to mate. That would have given them better standing in the pack also, but it would never have happened. If she'd had any notion that she had a chance to mate him after this happened, she had to know she'd blown it.

He carried Letta into the healer's hut and the healer hurried to take care of Letta's injuries. Tomas brought Gia in and laid her down on another bed, looking furious that Letta would get special treatment when Gia had been a pack member all along.

The healer continued to work on Letta, removing her bandages, cleaning her wounds, and wrapping them with clean bandages when Myla finally made it to the hut. Simon asked her if she was all right.

"Yeah, thanks, Simon. I'm just tired, but I was worried about Letta," Myla said.

"Gia is a member of this pack," Tomas said, their other brothers trying to come into the healer's hut to see her.

Ronan said, "Everyone, out, except for the injured women, our pack leader, and Myla." He shut the door on their exodus.

Simon heard all the grumbling outside and knew he'd have to call a pack council meeting as soon as he was sure that Letta would pull through. "How is she?" he asked the healer.

"As injured as Myla had been, I'm afraid. I wish I could use Letta's healing abilities to help. Will she stay with us, or will you send her away so she isn't killed by one of our own?" The healer sounded just as irritated that Gia would do this to Letta and glanced in Gia's direction with a hateful glower.

Gia scowled at Simon. "Okay, listen, I believed she was running off and so I followed her. I thought the collar was supposed to stop her, so I just continued to follow her, thinking she'd scream in pain and turn around. But it didn't stop her. She just kept going."

"You waited long enough. You could have returned and told me Letta had run off," Simon said.

"It would have taken too long. I barked at her to stop. I shifted and pleaded with her to return."

"Why didn't you stop her right away? Closer to the village?" Simon asked, knowing all Gia's words were lies.

"I thought the collar would work!"

"How dumb do you think my brother is?" Myla sounded as furious as Simon felt.

"Do I get to tell my story, or what?" Gia directed the question to Simon as if Myla had no business saying anything.

"Go ahead." For what it was worth. Simon knew Gia had waited until Letta was far enough away that her howls wouldn't reach far enough for anyone in the village to hear her. The only reason they heard her howls, crying for help, was that he'd already discovered Letta missing and he and several other male wolves had been racing to find her. Then he and the other wolves had realized Gia was following her and he'd figured nothing good could have come of that.

He knew the confrontation between the women wouldn't have ended well. The healer did all she could for Letta and began to take care of Gia's wounds.

"Anyway, the scorpion fae turned and growled at me, teeth bared. She has some notion you want her for a mate," Gia said. "And because of that, she attacked me, thinking I had a chance with you. I hadn't provoked her in the least. I wouldn't have. She's an unproven wolf in her fighting skills and I was afraid she'd be seriously injured if we sparred. What was I supposed to do? She attacked, and I had to defend myself. I was only trying to injure her enough to get her to stop attacking me."

"She howled for help," Simon reminded Gia.

"She only did so as a ploy to make it sound as though she was the innocent one. She's a devious scorpion fae. They're dark of heart. They killed their own people. Everyone knows that." Gia took a deep, steadying breath. "She set the whole thing up. I didn't realize she knew I was following her until it was nearly too late. She waited until we were so far away that I couldn't howl and reach anyone for help."

"As if you would," Myla said. "I don't believe a word you say."

Glancing at his sister, Simon tilted his head to the

side, telling his sister to stay out of it, no matter how good her intentions were. He didn't want her making an enemy of Gia also, though he suspected it was too late for that.

"Normally, I *wouldn't* have howled for help. You're right. I would have handled it, like an alpha would. Like a potential leader would," Gia said. "I wouldn't have howled, looking to be protected like some little beta wolf. Or pretended that I was the innocent one, needing to be rescued."

Letta groaned and Simon quickly took her hand. "How are you feeling, Letta?"

Myla was at her side too, taking her free hand. "You're safe now."

"As if I'm the big, bad wolf," Gia said, sarcastically.

Letta glanced at Gia. "Sorry for your injuries. You shouldn't have attacked me and I wouldn't have had to defend myself."

Scowling, Gia snorted. "Ha! Make up a story, why don't you."

"You're the one who's made up a story." Letta turned to Simon. "I don't have to stay here, do I?"

"Maybe in a cage," Gia said, as if she had any say in it.

"We'll move you to our cottage, Letta," Simon said. "Myla, can you watch over her there? Or do you need to rest and Ronan can watch over her?"

"I'll be fine. I can take care of her."

"You can stay here," Simon said to Gia, and then he

lifted Letta in his arms and carried her out of the healer's hut.

"I'll come check on Letta later," the healer called out to them.

"I'm so sorry," Simon said to Letta.

She didn't say anything.

"I shouldn't have put the collar on you." Simon couldn't believe Gia would stalk Letta down and attack her.

"It didn't knock me out." Letta gave him a small smile of victory.

Glad she didn't seem angry with him that Gia could have killed her, Simon smiled down at her. Then Myla opened the door to their cottage for him.

He carried Letta into the room that was now hers and laid her in the bed, and then Myla covered her with a blanket.

"I'll be here to get you anything you need," Myla said.

Simon cleared his throat. "I need to leave. I have to speak with the council. But I wanted to ask before I go, why did you leave, Letta?"

"I wasn't leaving you and Myla or the pack. I was going to see if Ena or Brett could remove my collar and then I was returning here to gloat."

Simon nearly laughed, except that this was so serious, he shook his head instead. He removed the collar from around her neck, wishing he'd done so earlier. All that had mattered at the time was that she was brought home to have her injuries taken care of.

"We don't want you to leave us," Myla said.

"She's right," Simon said. "I'll be back in a while." He left the cottage and stalked through the woods to the council hut.

Ronan had already alerted the elders of the council as to the problem between the two she-wolves, so they had gathered, and he was guarding the council hut for the moment. Simon thanked him and entered the hut, then closed the door.

"You can send her away," Argos, the leader of the council said.

"Her brothers would object," Simon said.

Argos lifted a brow. "The scorpion fae has brothers also?"

Simon let out his breath in exasperation. He had suspected who Argos had meant by saying Simon should send her away, but he wasn't allowing Argos, or anyone on the council, to change his mind about this. The only way he'd let Letta go was if she didn't want to remain with them, and who could blame her?

"You know very well who I mean. Any wolf who injured one of our own would be banished, unless there was good evidence the wolf was acting in its own defense," Simon said.

"Gia's brothers say the scorpion fae attacked her first."

"Gia's words against Letta's," Simon said. "I can tell you that Letta didn't start the fight and that Gia had no intention of returning Letta to the pack. She had every intention of finishing her off before we could rescue Letta. Why would Letta attack Gia?"

"Gia wanted to please you, so when she learned the scorpion fae had run off, she tried to convince Letta to return with her," Argos said.

"So she nearly kills Letta? Letta is new to our ways. No one has taught her how to fight as a wolf. What would she gain by taking on Gia?" Simon knew the council members understood the right of it, but he was also certain they worried about the consequences of Gia's actions and if Simon banished her, her brothers would go too.

They were good fighting men, and had been loyal, up to this point.

"I would never have mated Gia, even if Letta had not come to our village. Gia doesn't get along with most of the she-wolves in the pack," Simon said.

Beatrice, the only woman on his council of five, agreed. "She minds herself when she's around your sisters and me," she said. "The younger she-wolves, she has nothing to do with, nor does she with the older ones. But when it comes to eligible she-wolves..." Beatrice shook her head. "I've counseled her numerous times over her behavior. If she sees you are remotely interested in or friendly to an eligible female and she learns of it, the wolf will have to deal with Gia's wrath."

"Why has nobody said anything about this to me?" Simon knew she wasn't pleasant with the other she-wolves, but he hadn't known she would bully them.

"The strongest of us leads," Beatrice said. "If she became your mate, then you and she could make a powerful team."

"If I ever learn you know something like this about the pack members, and you don't keep me informed, you'll be removed from the council." Simon was furious. No wolf would bully other wolves in his pack. Yes, in the wild, the wolves that were not fae wolf shifters, did, but he needed his pack to work as a cohesive team, a family.

Beatrice inclined her head, acknowledging his ruling.

"So now do you see?" he asked the others on the council. "Gia has had it in for Letta from the beginning."

"She's a scorpion fae," Argos said.

"She's a wolf shifter like us. And she's a healer. Not to mention she has some special skills none of us have. She could be an asset. Many of our people have welcomed her to the pack for saving Myla." Simon paced in front of his council members. He knew they'd have heartburn over sending Gia away, and her brothers following her, but he wasn't sending Letta away.

"She ran." Steel was Simon's age, the youngest man on the council, everyone else gray-haired and much respected by the pack. Though he was just as respected for his just and fair opinions. Simon had included him on the council to help represent a younger point-of-view. "The scorpion—"

Simon gave him such a sharp look, Steel corrected himself, "Letta. She ran. Why would you want her back? Send her to the dragon shifter fae. The princess wants her. Let her deal with her."

"She wasn't running away," Simon said. Everyone looked at him with disbelief. He didn't blame them, since he'd thought the same thing until she told him why she had left. "She was going to find Ena and see if she, or one of her staff, could remove the collar. And then she was returning here to prove I couldn't control her. She wants to stay with us."

The council members exchanged looks.

"I'm sorry," Beatrice said. "I should have told you about Gia's actions before this."

Simon nodded. "After what Gia pulled with Letta, and after hearing Beatrice's testimony, how Gia's reacted to other females in the pack, I would feel compelled to banish her. But the consideration must be made concerning her brothers. So here's my recommendation. We keep Gia in the pack, with a stern warning that if she intimidates any she-wolf in the pack, she'll be banished. The same goes for Gia's brothers, if they attempt to hassle Letta in any way. Letta stays with the pack, unless she chooses to leave. If Gia starts a fight with Letta, she's banished."

"What if Letta starts a fight with Gia?" Steel asked.

"I'll deal with it."

"You can't be thinking of taking the wolf as your mate," Argos said. "She's a—"

"Wolf shifter like us." It didn't mean that Simon was going to, but he wanted them to know that he was open to the notion, if she was interested too, at some point in time. He couldn't even believe he was considering it.

All of his council members were each mulling that over, and he knew that they realized she could be their co-pack leader, so they'd better treat her well. Not that she would treat them badly, if they didn't, but karma could bite them back.

Usually, when they had a situation of this magnitude, his council members made recommendations first, and then he told them what he was going to do. This time, he couldn't help jumping in with both feet and telling it like it was going to be from the beginning. He knew they would have defended Gia's actions over a wolf who hadn't belonged to the pack all these years. "Do you have any other concerns or suggestions?"

Steel cast Simon a small smile. "You do realize if you keep her, Letta, in the pack, you might have some bachelor wolf fights over her."

Simon figured that. He guessed that no one had shown Gia much interest because they thought Simon and she might become mated. Maybe now, they would make an attempt and she'd become mated and the rivalry would end between her and Letta.

"You?" Simon asked his friend.

Steel just smiled.

Simon smiled darkly.

No one else on the council had a thing to say, and he

figured they assumed his mind was already made up as far as where this would go. It was.

Ronan was outside, keeping any wolves away from overhearing what was being said inside the council hut. Wolves had such good hearing, that it was important to keep the council meeting private until all was decided. Concerning his decision, Simon would tell the parties involved, Gia and her brothers first, and then Letta. After that, Argos would let the rest of the pack know that no wolf would badger any other wolves in the pack.

When Simon left the council hut and headed to the healer's hut to talk with Gia and her brothers, he overheard Gia's brothers talking inside the hut about what they would do if Simon kicked Gia out. They would fight him to take over the pack, leave and gather their own pack first, or try to convince him to change his mind, let Gia pay for the consequences of her actions, or all leave and they wouldn't look back.

Simon opened the door. When Simon entered the healer's hut, the brothers cast him superior looks. Gia appeared worn out, good one on her.

Simon explained what he'd decided, prefacing it with, "We've known each other from the time we were young pups, and I'd hate for something like this to come between us. Gia will remain in the pack. If you agree with my decision, we go on about our business. We'll give the women a chance to heal, and from there, if they choose to be friends, it's up to them. But no more fighting between the two of you."

"What if she starts—" Gia began to say.

Simon raised his hand to stop her objection. "We fight as a unit, always ready for the worst-case scenario, and no fighting within our ranks. If you badger any female, you're banished, Gia. If you have issue with my ruling, tell me now."

The men all shook their heads, looking relieved they didn't have to leave the pack because of their sister's shenanigans. But Tomas was smiling a little, and Simon wondered what was up with that. He had known him forever, so he could pretty much guess what he was thinking. Not this time.

Simon bowed his head to them in agreement and they did the same to him, all but Gia. She was one obstinate wolf, who reminded Simon a lot of another. *Hannah.*

Simon left the healer's hut then and headed for his own cottage to speak with Letta and prayed she was doing better. But when he arrived, he found her sound asleep.

"What has been decided?" Myla asked.

"Gia and her brothers will stay, but no more infractions of the rules. Did you know that Gia was giving some of our she-wolves a hard time?"

"No. Who said she was? I mean, I know she snaps at some of the she-wolves, but I've never seen her get physical with them. She doesn't dare do anything like that with me. Mostly, I'm sure, because I'm your sister, have your confidence, and I'm no threat to her in the mating department."

"Beatrice is the one who finally said so. She's been warned also that if she withholds information about something this important, she could find herself dismissed from the council. And Steel is testing me."

"Oh? How?"

"He intends to court Letta."

Myla sighed. "Does he not realize he won't win against you?"

Simon smiled. "Who says I'm in the running?"

Myla took his arm and led him into the kitchen. "Because I know you, dear brother. Help me make lunch. It is time and Letta was going to help me, but she's now indisposed."

CHAPTER 10

The next day, Letta was sitting in the living room, a blanket on her lap, receiving several wolves, male and female, who came by to wish her well and to welcome her to the pack as if she was visiting royalty. She was glad to see the outpouring of friendship from the wolves, when she'd been afraid they might have believed Gia's lies.

When the last of the wolves had left Myla and Simon's cottage, Myla brought Letta and herself a cup of jasmine tea and sat down again in the living room.

"You have made many friends among the wolves of our pack. It didn't hurt that Simon learned what Gia was doing to some of the she-wolves and put a stop to it. They know you're the reason for helping them out." Myla sounded proud of her. "I believe Gia is in the proverbial doghouse and no one wants to be treated that way. She's been trying to convince whoever will listen that you were the aggressor and she was defending herself. I don't think anyone believes her. Not when they know her better than that."

"Do you think she will try to kill me again?" Letta really needed to learn how to fight better as a wolf.

"I think she'll want to, but she may feel it's too risky. And if she did kill you, Simon, and most everyone else, would look at her as the prime suspect."

Someone knocked on the door, and Myla went to get it. When she opened the door, she frowned. "Tomas. Simon isn't here."

Letta knew Tomas was one of Gia's brothers and definitely not her friend.

"I didn't come here to see him. I'd like to speak with Letta, if I may," Tomas said to Myla.

Why? To apologize for his sister's rotten behavior toward her? No thanks. Gia would have to do the apologizing, and Letta suspected she'd rather die than do that.

"Let me see if she wishes to speak with you." Myla closed the door and whispered to Letta, "Do you want to see him?"

Letta nodded. She figured she needed to make an effort to be friendly with Gia and her brothers, if it was at all possible, since she was going to stay with the wolf pack. If Tomas was offering a chance at conciliation, she'd accept it. She suspected he was in charge of his brothers but didn't have much control over his sister.

Myla opened the door. "Come in, Tomas. I don't

think you need introductions." Myla made him some tea and then took a seat nearby, watching over the situation, being protective of Letta.

Letta so appreciated her for it.

Tomas sat on a chair opposite the couch where Letta was sitting. "First, I want to apologize for my sister's behavior."

"That she attacked me without provocation." Letta wanted to make it clear to Tomas that if he was apologizing for his sister, he knew just what he was apologizing for.

"Uh, yes."

"Good. Thank you. I'm glad you understand the truth of the matter."

"Right, well, I don't feel it's enough to just apologize to you, considering how badly you were injured." Tomas was eyeing her with what she thought was something akin to interest, but Letta wasn't buying it.

"How badly *she* injured me." Letta could see a pattern of Tomas downplaying his sister's actions.

"Right. To make up for it, to show you we harbor no ill feelings toward you, I wish to court you."

Myla nearly dropped her cup of tea.

Letta snapped her gaping mouth closed. She finally found her tongue and said, "That's very sweet of you, and I feel most honored, really." *Not.* She figured just where Tomas was coming from—allow him to court her and then Gia would be free to change Simon's mind about courting her. Letta wasn't a scorpion fae without some of her own resources. She could be just as wily as a wolf. And she wasn't going to be outmaneuvered. Of course, it might mean that she was going to make an enemy of Tomas and the rest of the siblings. But she didn't believe she was anything but, anyway. "But…I've agreed to court Simon. If things don't work out between us though, I'll definitely consider your proposal."

Myla looked surprised to hear Letta say that. Letta wondered then if she really thought her brother had. She would have to tell her it was all just a ploy, but that she would straighten it out with Simon when he returned to the cottage.

Tomas's face turned red. "Simon has said nothing of this to anyone."

"I'm sure he didn't want to mention it until we had our first few dates, after I heal up, of course."

Myla was quiet, watching the emotions play across Tomas's face: surprise, disbelief, annoyance.

Tomas abruptly stood. "I'll see myself out." He didn't say he wanted to see her if it didn't work out between her and Simon. She was certain he would be miffed at anyone for turning him down for a chance at a courtship. She was certain he wouldn't want to truly go through with a mating either, just wait until his sister had what she wanted. Tomas hurried for the door and let himself out.

Hadn't he ever been rejected before? Letta smiled and finished her tea.

Myla smiled at her and waited for Tomas to shut the door before she spoke.

Simon entered the cottage right after Tomas left. "What was that all about? Was he giving you trouble?" he asked Letta, looking ready to run out of the cottage and take Tomas to task.

"Tomas apologized for his sister attacking Letta, unprovoked," Myla said.

"Good." Simon shut the door and joined them.

"And he asked her if he could court her," Myla said.

"What?" Simon appeared as astonished as they'd been to hear Tomas's proposal.

"Letta thanked him but said *you're* courting her." Myla seemed amused and pleased.

Simon frowned. "What?" He turned his attention to Letta, but she thought he only looked surprised, not angry with her over it.

Letta and Myla smiled at him.

Simon let out his breath. "I was going to ask how you're feeling, but it appears that you are doing well enough to cause great mischief."

Letta would have laughed, except she wasn't sure if Simon was exasperated with her or angry or resigned. "What would you have me say? Yes, I'll court you Tomas? And then what? He would only do so to get me out of the way so that Gia could get on your good side."

"Which is not happening."

"Okay, but if I flat-out refused his offer, he could take the rejection as an insult. But if I were courting you, or even your brother Aegis, or Ronan, since both have asked me already—"

"You can't be serious." Simon appeared as though he couldn't believe it.

"She is serious. I heard them both ask her. But she told them she couldn't court anyone right away. They said it figured—first interesting she-wolf in ages and you get her." Myla fixed Simon some tea.

"They don't seem to mind that I'm a scorpion fae." Letta straightened out the blanket on her lap.

"You're a wolf-shifter fae," Simon reminded her. "I can't believe you told Tomas we're courting."

"We don't have to be. We could have broken up already." Letta shrugged. "I can still date one of your brothers."

"No, the word will have spread through the pack in record time. Everyone's been waiting for me to get on the ball and mate a wolf." Simon let out his breath as if he were exasperated with her. "How are you doing?"

"I'm feeling better, but I'm tired."

"You need to return to bed." He helped her to back to bed and covered her up.

"Are you upset with me about what I said to Tomas? I really didn't want to cause you trouble. You don't have to court me."

Simon sat down on the bed, smiled, and took her hand. "To tell you the truth, I just thought *I* was going to be the one asking *you*...first."

"You took too long."

He chuckled. "As soon as you're feeling better, I'll take you out to dinner. Not here though. We'll go to this restaurant I know in the human world."

"Is that where you take all your dates?"

"Never there. My sisters and brothers and I have gone there a number of times. Great steaks and side dishes."

"Sounds good. I'll be ready."

"Get your sleep."

***

Three days later, Myla and Letta were practicing play wolf-fights, despite Simon's concern that Letta wasn't completely healed. But she'd been insistent that she be allowed to practice. So he'd finally agreed. Myla had assured him privately that she'd take it really easy with Letta and he knew she would to protect her friend.

He went to Ronan's place to talk to Mark and Bryan to see how they were faring. They'd been doing really well with their shifting, practicing play fights with Simon's brothers, and learning to fae travel short distances. They were happy they were fae now, and not just humans in the fae world. They could transport on their own and not need help getting to other locations. Simon imagined when they were helping the dragons to fight their battles, it was rather inconvenient to all concerned. Simon still wondered if they would suddenly become another type of fae, the kind that they should have been born with. And if so, which fae would they prefer living with? He hoped it wasn't a kind of fae that didn't get along with the wolf shifters.

"Hey, brother," Simon said, when Ronan opened the door for him. "How are things going?"

"Well, Mark and Bryan are fighting in the clearing down by the river."

"Right. They wanted to learn how to wolf fight," Simon said.

"I don't mean that," Ronan said. "Mark mentioned that the queen wanted Bryan to create her gardens for her, to pay for his hospital visit, but since he had been turned, she gave the job to Mark."

"Okay."

"So they're fighting over it, because it comes with a royal title." Ronan smiled.

Simon shook his head.

"But I've been thinking we should let them go. The dragon shifters can bring them back here, if they have any trouble with them. And if they want to return to the pack, they're welcome to. Anytime."

"All right. We can do that. A couple of our guys can go with them to make sure it's okay with the dragons. Where are Myla and Letta?" Simon asked.

"They're practicing wolf fights and practice hunting out in the field near where the guys are. Aegis and Tomas are with them. What are we going to do about Hannah?"

Simon knew he'd have to make a decision about her soon. No one objected to her staying confined in the cage still. They let her out for exercise and eating, but if someone couldn't keep an eye on her, they put her back in a cage. For now, no one wanted to take her in either. That was his main concern. Someone had to watch her.

His brothers had been happy to have Mark and Bryan staying with them, and the guys had been agreeable and helpful with any of the pack duties they needed to do. So his brothers had no problem with taking them in.

"I'll go see them," Simon said.

"I wish Mark and Bryan would stay with us, but if they have their heart set on going back to the dragon fae territory, then that's where they should be allowed to go," Ronan said.

"I agree. They'll always be welcome to return here. The wolf pack is their family now. I'll see you in a little bit."

"Hey, Letta said you were courting her. But you haven't started taking her anywhere yet. Let me know if you change your mind. I want to take her out before our brothers have a chance to ask her out."

Simon smiled. "Don't hold your breath."

"I knew you'd say that. I'll go with you," Ronan said.

Then they left to find Mark and Bryan. When they finally reached the clearing where they were, Simon was surprised to actually see his sister and Letta play-fighting as wolves close to the river, even though his brother said they were out there. It was just seeing the women fighting that had his heart pounding.

He watched them while they played, practicing

lunges and feints, biting gently, barking, growling, and having fun. Then he smiled. He could watch them for hours. Even Mark, Bryan, and Aegis were sitting on their rumps in wolf form, watching the she-wolves sparring.

Then the women saw Simon watching them and stopped playing.

"I came to see Mark and Bryan but enjoyed watching you ladies too." To the men, Simon said, "Ronan said that the two of you want to go back to the dragon fae kingdom. I'll have my brothers take you."

The men shifted. "All right," Mark said. "I'll work for Ena. Bryan was supposed to work for the queen. But we want to come back here and keep learning more about our wolf abilities. It won't be the same while we're with the dragon fae as it has been being here among the rest of you."

"Yeah, I feel the same way. Maybe we can even find mates among your wolves," Bryan said, smiling. "Eventually."

"Okay it's decided then. You can leave today," Simon said, glad they were considering returning to the pack. It always helped to have good and able pack members, especially if they lost Tomas and his brothers at some future date because of the tenable situation with Gia.

"What about Hannah?" Bryan asked. "Can we take her back with us?"

"Ena doesn't want her back. Otherwise, I'd happily send her along with you. Would the queen take her?"

Simon asked. He'd rather Hannah live somewhere else. *Anywhere* else. He'd left her locked up, but only because he still felt she would be out-of-control, and it was punishment for attacking the others. But he knew he needed to give her a chance.

Bryan shook his head. "No. Ena's the one who is always taking in problem people. If Ena doesn't want Hannah returned, she can't go there."

"I will take responsibility for her," Ronan finally said.

Aegis let out his breath. "That means I'm stuck with her too."

Simon smiled. "It's decided then. She stays with the two of you, under strict orders to do everything you say. Any infraction, she returns to the cage."

Letta and Myla shifted.

"Myla, are you okay with this? I should have asked you first," Simon said.

"Yes. She needs to have a chance to prove she's going to be a viable member of the pack."

"All right then. I'll release Hannah and set up the rules for her," Simon said.

They all headed back to the village then. Simon, along with Ronan, Aegis, Mark, and Bryan, went in to the hut to speak with Hannah.

"I'm releasing you to Ronan and Aegis's care. You'll have to listen to what they tell you. You'll be watched until you learn how to behave. Agreed?" Simon asked.

"Yeah."

"All right." Simon unlocked the cage and she came out of it.

"So I'll be staying with Mark and Bryan too? Since they're staying at Ronan and Aegis's cottage?" Hannah asked.

"No," Bryan said. "We're returning to the dragon fae kingdom. Ena won't take you back. We told you over and over again how you needed to straighten up." Bryan sounded angry with her for her acting up so much when she had lived at Ena's castle.

"Well, it's too late now, I guess," Hannah said flippantly.

Simon just shook his head. "Okay, well, you go with Aegis to the cottage. And Ronan, if you would, have a couple of our wolves go with Mark and Bryan to the dragon fae kingdom."

After that, Simon went to see Letta and Myla at the cottage before Myla could make plans for dinner for them. "Are you ready for a dinner date, Letta?"

She smiled. "I sure am."

"Change into your human clothes, if you have any, and we'll leave."

"I do. Though I'd love to go shopping for more, now that I'm more settled," Letta said.

Myla smiled brightly. "If Simon doesn't want to take you shopping, I will."

CHAPTER 11

Shopping was not something Simon liked to do, but he could go with the women to offer protection, in case they ran into fae-seers in the human world. Some other time though. For now, he wanted everyone to know that he truly was dating Letta.

Once he had dressed in jeans and a shirt, Letta came out of her room wearing a little black dress. He was expecting her to wear jeans too, so he was glad to see her dressed so nicely.

"I'll take you to the parking lot near the back of the steakhouse to avoid anyone seeing us, hopefully, when we pop in." Not that the fae were averse to shocking humans. It was part of who they were.

"All right. I'm ready."

He took her hand and transported them in the way of the fae, except once they were out of Myla's sight and enveloped in darkness, he pulled Letta into his arms. And kissed her.

He could tell the way Letta seemed so awkward, she'd never been kissed before, and he knew then that she had told the truth: that if she'd wanted to find a mate, she had to leave her clan.

He was just fortunate enough to be the first. She leaned into the kiss then, and he felt his thoughts swirling with possibility. She was darkness and light. Beautiful, strong, and courageous. And she seemed to like him, despite their rocky beginning, as much as he cared about her.

And then he realized they were kissing still, her lips pressed against his, her arms wrapped around his neck, and his around her waist, a brass lamp shedding light on them.

She suddenly pulled her mouth away from his, her cheeks flushing. "We're here."

He smiled. "We sure are." He took her hand and began to escort her to the restaurant. "I love their steaks here. They have the best food." Even the aroma of steaks grilling filled the air, lured them in.

She was about to say something when Tomas and his brothers suddenly appeared in front of them.

That didn't bode well. They wouldn't have followed them here, unless they'd planned to create problems.

"Trouble," Letta said under her breath.

"Yeah. No doubt."

He saw the fae collars they were carrying, but before the men could grab Simon and Letta, or they could transport away, she cast a pale white mist all over each of the men. They stopped dead in their tracks and Simon wondered if she'd frozen them in place. She pulled Simon into the darkness, and he knew she was fae transporting him somewhere, but home? Or somewhere else?

"What did you do to them?" Simon asked, as she wrapped her arms around him. She couldn't leave them frozen there in the parking lot.

"I did what they were going to do to us. Removed their ability to fae transport. They were only frozen for a few seconds, giving us time to get away."

"You used magic." He smiled down at her.

"I hope it's all right." But Letta sounded that she didn't care if it was or not, she wasn't allowing the brothers to get the best of them.

"Yeah, it was a great move. Where are we going?"

"To one of *my* favorite restaurants. Seafood and steaks on the ocean."

He chuckled. "Now this is what I call a date." They stood on a pier, looking out at the ocean, whitecaps on the water sparkling as the waves crested, the sun setting, casting a gold and orange glow over the edge of the world and off the clouds clinging to the sky above. It couldn't have been more perfect.

Then they went inside and got a table as if they were royalty, convincing the hostess they were ahead of everyone on the list. When the waiter offered them menus, they both ordered steak and lobster.

"You know, their sister probably knew all about what they were up to and will go fetch them, once they don't return after a certain amount of time," Simon said.

Letta agreed. "I wonder how long they were supposed to be gone. If Gia thought it would be some time, then she may still be waiting for their return when we get back. She'll have to bring back one at a time though. Do you think she'll get any help with it?"

"That depends. If they think it has anything to do with causing trouble for you and me, no. They won't want to get on the wrong side of this." At least Simon didn't think so.

"What do you think they intended to do with us?"

"Not sure. Fae collar us and leave us there, maybe, but someone would have gotten suspicious if we hadn't returned after a couple of hours and come looking for us. Once they learned what the brothers had done, they'd have been in hot water. Tomas and his brothers might have planned to take us somewhere else and dump us. We would be stuck until we could find a way back to the restaurant before we were picked up. If they fae transported us somewhere, which they would have done if they were moving us somewhere else, no telling where we might have ended up. They might have even separated us. Or, they might have eliminated us, because they would know, if our people learned they had anything to do with our disappearance, they would be blamed and could have been killed for it. Ronan would take over the pack, if I didn't return. But he'd lead an investigation into what happened to us. I suspect, Tomas and his brothers want to take over the pack, though they'd have a fight on their hands."

"What are you going to do about them?"

Simon let out his breath. "You took away their ability to fae transport. They can't get it back, unless you give it back, correct? Or Gia fetches them?"

"Absolutely."

"Good. I'll decide when we return." He reached across the table and took her hand and caressed it. "I just want to enjoy this time with you."

"You may be regretting that I came into your lives."

"No way. Not after you saved Myla's life."

"I was afraid of what Alton might do to me because I had seen where his treasure was."

The meals arrived, and they began to carve up their steaks.

"Believe me, I was concerned also. I had no idea how he'd react. Once we knew you were a wolf, I'm sure that put his mind at ease. We don't need the gold for anything."

"But I'll need to earn my keep. I wondered about working for him, guarding the gold too."

"Not until you've had more training as a wolf. Myla's been taking it easy on you."

"Yeah, that's what I thought, but no matter how aggressively I fight back, she won't take me on."

He laughed. Letta was nowhere near being that aggressive. Though it was a sobering thought. Letta had been ill-equipped to fight Gia. He could see what a strong disadvantage she had just from the mistakes she'd made while play-fighting with Myla. Even Tomas had been there watching them, and Simon wondered if he'd wanted to see for himself how well Letta could fight.

"I could get one of your brothers to fight me."

"No." He smiled. "I'll help to train you so you can get the feel of a bigger wolf."

"Deal. Just promise me you won't make it too easy because that's what Myla's doing."

Simon chuckled. "I'm the alpha pack leader. How would it look if I let a new she-wolf take me down? I'll make you work for it."

She smiled. "Good, because I'm aiming to take you down."

***

When they returned to the wolf pack, Simon knew he'd have to deal with Tomas and Gia and their brothers for their deceitfulness. He hoped they hadn't convinced his people that Letta had spitefully taken their ability to transport home away from them. If they ditched the collars, they could say they just happened to go to that restaurant and it would be his and Letta's word against the brothers.

But when they arrived back at his cottage, Myla was wringing her hands and quickly said, "Gia's beside herself with fear. Fae seers have taken her brothers hostage at the restaurant where you and Letta went to eat. She just got back from there. Everyone thought there was something suspect about them being there in the first place and were getting ready to send a search party for you. Not to mention, since you were at the restaurant also, they were concerned you had been taken also. But Gia said you and Letta weren't there or she would have solicited your aid."

Though Simon didn't want a fae seer killing their kind, he assumed Tomas and the others had intended to kill him and Letta somewhere far away from the restaurant so no one would be the wiser.

"She said that her brothers couldn't fae transport to save themselves from the fae seers. She wasn't making any sense," Myla said.

"Letta, you stay here with Myla. I'll speak with Gia and take a couple of my brothers to help track them down."

"They were going to kill us or leave us to the same fate," Letta reminded him.

"Yes, I agree, but I need to deal with this here."

"What?" Myla asked, her eyes wide.

"Letta protected us when Gia's brothers tried to collar us."

"Then leave them there," Myla said, furious.

"I would if they were just stuck there, but if they've been taken by fae seers, I don't want the humans to harm them. I only believed they'd be stuck there for a while until Gia could return them home and then I'd decide what to do from there."

"How did they lose their ability to transport?" Myla

asked.

"My magic. And if I were to die, they'd never be able to fae transport," Letta said. "I'm the only one who can reverse it, and I'm going with you."

"Have you ever dealt with fae seers?" Simon asked, frowning at Letta. She seemed so sweet and innocent, and yet she had a real devious side to her. But he loved that she had reacted so quickly and saved them from whatever Tomas and his brothers had in store for them.

"I lived among the humans and I've dealt with my fair share of fae seers. My scorpion fae parents survived the great battle that destroyed our kind. When I was twelve, they took me to be raised among the few who were left in the forests where we became woodland fae. We lived with our king and other young fae. So yes, I have dealt with fae seers and humans of all kinds. But I have the advantage of having an arsenal of magic."

Just when he thought he knew all there was to know about Letta, there was more. She had an arsenal of magic? He just hoped he always stayed on her good side.

"All right, let's go," Simon said.

Myla looked hopeful she could go too, but Simon shook his head. "Just Aegis, Steel, and me, well, and Letta." Then they hurried off to find some of the men gathered in the common area.

Gia was trying to organize a search party when she saw Simon and Letta. Her skin paled and her eyes grew big.

"Surprised to see us, Gia? After your brothers tried

to collar us?" Simon had to let everyone gathered know what it was all about.

Gia closed her gaping mouth. He suspected she'd thought her brothers had already eliminated them. Or once Simon and Letta arrived here, she might have believed her brothers hadn't seen Simon and Letta before the fae seers grabbed them and they didn't know her brothers had even been there.

"I...I don't know what you're talking about." Gia looked stricken, probably worried Simon would leave them to their fates.

"Sure, you do. And you went to look for them because they were taking too long to return. Aegis, Steel, we're returning to the place where her brothers were captured."

"And Letta?" Ronan asked.

"Yes. We might be able to use her magic skills."

"And Gia?" Aegis asked, frowning at her.

"Yes. She can help save her brothers, if we can do so before we're too late. Ronan, you're in charge while I'm gone." Then Simon turned to Gia. "Show us where you last saw your brothers."

CHAPTER 12

Then they all transported to the steak restaurant and followed their trail to the parking lot. After that, their fae dust trail was gone.

"They must have carried them off in a vehicle." Letta pointed to the building. "See the security cameras on the restaurant under the eaves? We can check the security videos and see who took the brothers. With any luck, we can locate the vehicle soon."

They all vanished and headed inside the restaurant and found the office and went inside. A middle-aged man was working on a computer.

Simon said, "Four men were taken hostage in your parking lot."

"What? Who are you? You can't be in here. I'm calling the police."

Letta waved her hand over the man's face. "Show us the video for the last two hours. Hurry. Your life depends on it."

The man quickly did what they asked and Simon was again in awe of what Letta could do. Here she had the ability to force him or anyone else to open the cage and release her and she didn't. Unless she could only do that to humans and not the fae.

Once they saw the blue van grab Tomas and his brothers and drive off, they were able to identify his license. But how were they going to find the vehicle now?

They left the restaurant before anyone else discovered their unauthorized visit to the security office.

"Any ideas?" Simon asked Letta, because she seemed to know how to deal more with situations like this since she'd lived in the human's world for some time while growing up.

"We just have to call into the police station and get them to give us their address."

"Using your magic. But don't you have to do it in person?" Simon asked.

"No. I'm just that good." Letta glanced at Gia as if letting her know that she shouldn't mess with her any longer.

Simon was impressed.

When Letta pulled out a cell phone, he was surprised.

"I swiped it off the guy in the office." Letta looked for something on the phone, then made a call. "Hi, I need the name of the owner and the address of—" She hung up the phone.

"What are you doing?" Simon asked.

"The van's here. Right there. Maybe they believe this is a place where our kind congregate." Letta said to Gia, "Did they see you before?"

"Yeah."

"Okay, so they knew you'd go for reinforcements and we're it," Letta said.

Simon cast Gia an annoyed look. "You could have told us that before."

"So we vanish," Gia said. "Transport before they can take us prisoner."

Three men got out of the van, eyeing the fae with speculation.

"Nope. We take them prisoner. Or...I should say, I do." Letta warned them, "They have Taser guns."

Before the three men could get close enough to shoot the fae, Letta cast a spell, making them freeze. "Okay, come on. Let's take them in their van and learn where they took the brothers."

"What did you do to them?" Gia sounded irritated. "They can't speak or do anything."

"They will, once they get in the van." Letta grabbed one of the men's arms and dragged him with her. Even though he couldn't do anything to them, he could still stumble along.

Once all of them were in the van, Letta said to the man she'd made sit in the driver's seat, "Drive us to where you took the fae."

"Wait, you don't think he's going to really take us there, do you?" Gia asked.

"It wasn't just an order," Letta said. "He's compelled to do it. He has no choice. And if you want to leave, just…leave."

Gia shut up then.

"Are the fae alive?" Letta asked one of the other men.

"Yeah, but we'll take 'em out and do away with them."

"You know you're a fae too, don't you? You just don't have your powers yet." Just in case it was true, Letta let that sink in.

Not that they really were, Simon was thinking.

"No," both the men muttered.

"Think about it. You can see the fae. Why? Humans can't. You just haven't come into your abilities yet. We have several former fae seers in our world who are now full fae. They're lucky they didn't kill any of our kind or they would never have been able to join us," Letta said.

Simon wasn't sure that was really true. Especially not in Hannah's case. He knew Brett had only killed an unseelie fae, the really bad news for their own kind, the seelie fae. Even Bryan and Mark might have killed the fae.

"As if we want to join you," one of the fae seers said.

Letta turned to look at them from the front passenger's seat. "If you start showing a fae aura, you'll be left to deal with the fae seers here. And you won't know how to go to our world. Just saying."

Simon wasn't about to take these men home with him, just to see if they were fae. Once they'd taken his own wolf pack members—rotten as they'd been—hostage, they were on their own, if they turned into the fae later on.

They drove about half an hour and ended up in the country at a red farmhouse. It looked warm and inviting, not like it could be a fae seer's fae killing ground. Chickens were running around, a couple of cows grazing in a pasture, two goats penned in another enclosure, very countrified.

"Where are the fae?" Simon asked.

"In the red barn, chained up. They'll be drowned in the river nearby and then buried," the driver said, as if he didn't get it that they were no longer in charge of the fae here.

"So what do we do with the fae seers?" Gia said. "If I was in charge, they would die."

"They could be just like us," Letta said. "Our king taught us to try and spread the word to their kind, whenever we could, to let them know that they could be in even more trouble if they end up having a fae aura and now they're the target for the fae seers."

"A scorpion fae? You've got to be kidding," Gia said.

"Propaganda," the driver said.

"Fact. We have a fae seer who is now a dragon-shifter fae prince. Another who is a dragon fae princess.

And three fae who can shift into wolves." Simon wasn't about to tell them that two of them had been human until a wolf shifter bit them.

"Wolf shifters? Like werewolves? Give me a break," one of the men in the back of the van said.

Aegis turned into a wolf and snarled at them. Mouths agape, the two humans shut up.

"You don't want to see the dragon shifters in a foul mood," Simon said.

His brother shifted back.

"Who else is here," Letta asked.

"Two of my brothers," the driver said. "They're watching the fae."

"What are you going to do with them?" Letta asked Simon.

Simon wanted to terminate them. But Letta was right. What if they were fae? Still, he wasn't about to allow them to remain here, preying on the fae kind. "How many more of you are in the area that can see us?"

"Just us five."

"We take them with us," Simon said. Though he didn't mean to keep them in his territory. He'd dump them somewhere and let them fend for themselves until they either became fae, or could befriend the fae, if that was possible. On the other hand, that could have happened to Princess Alicia, Prince Brett, and Mark and Bryan, all of whom Simon genuinely liked. Hannah was a different story. He couldn't believe he was agreeing with Letta on this, but she smiled at him as if pleased that he'd decided this. He was like Gia and couldn't see that the scorpion fae would feel this way about murdering fae seers. Maybe the scorpion fae had turned over a new leaf. Maybe a whole forest of them.

They left the van then, Letta making the three fae seers lead the way.

"Call your brothers out. Tell them you have another fae."

"Hey, Douglas, Bill! We got another fae!" the driver said.

The two men came out of the barn, looking eager to take the new fae hostage and Letta froze them.

"Okay, what do we do with Gia's brothers, since they're also guilty of a crime against us?" Letta asked.

"By my earlier ruling, if any of them attempted to harm you, they would be banished from the pack. I doubt any pack would want to give them refuge. If they had planned to eliminate us, as we suspect, they would have earned the death penalty. But I have another proposition. You've removed their ability to fae transport. After a year, if we've had no trouble with them, you can give their ability back. A year to prove they're loyal to me and you and the rest of the pack. A year to learn from their mistake."

"You can't do that!" Gia said.

Simon scowled at her, knowing that she was the one who had instigated it. "Letta can, and she will. And if anything happens to her, in the meantime, they will never have the ability to fae transport again. You know I have every right to terminate them for what they pulled with us."

Gia looked outraged.

"You too," Simon added.

Gia's expression fell. He wanted her to know that he saw her as guilty as the rest.

"Since you were involved too, I can do the same for you, remove your fae transport abilities, if you'd like," Letta said.

Gia quickly shook her head.

"Come on. Let's take the brothers home and we'll transport these guys afterwards." Simon headed for the barn.

"You could just give my brothers' transport powers back and then we could all leave at the same time. You wouldn't have to return for the humans," Gia reasoned.

"They're not getting their abilities back," Simon said. "Not for a year. If they want to transport anywhere, you'll have to take them, unless someone else agrees to carry them."

Then they went into the barn, the five fae seers following them, and Simon suspected that Letta's spell caused them to see her as their leader. Not a bad ability to have, really.

They saw the brothers had been beaten, bruised and bloodied. Simon wanted to do the same with the fae seers, but, again, he reminded himself that the brothers would have either killed him and Letta or left them to their fate with the fae seers themselves.

The wolf brothers all looked sheepish, hanging their heads when Simon, his brother, a council member, and Letta had come to rescue them.

"Free the fae," Letta told the fae seers.

They hurried to unchain the wolf brothers.

"You're not going to let them live, are you?" Tomas asked, his right eye swollen shut.

"Let's go." Simon wasn't about to explain his actions to Tomas. In fact, Simon figured if Tomas and his brothers remained in the pack, the rest of the wolves would frown on what they'd done here today. They could be real outcasts among the wolves. Gia also.

Each of them took ahold of one of the brothers, all but Letta. "Did you want me to take a fae seer?"

"No, we'll come back for them." Simon didn't want anyone to know where he took them, so that none of the brothers would attempt to kill them.

Then the wolves returned home with the brothers.

He told them what would happen with their abilities. Then, still leaving Ronan in charge, Simon, Letta, Aegis, Steel, and Myla returned for the five men.

"Where are we taking them?" Aegis asked. "Surely, you can't mean to take them to our village. The rest of our pack would find a reason to kill the fae seers."

"No. I was thinking, since Letta says her king is trying to make peace with these people, we could leave them there with him. He can decide what to do with them." Simon wasn't sure that would meet with the scorpion king's approval, but he thought since the king had suggested it, they'd give it a try.

Letta smiled. "I agree. He can put his speeches into practice."

When they finally arrived at the camp where King Tameron and his scorpion fae resided, he appeared surprised to see them, and that Letta would be the one who brought all of them there. "Letta."

Like Letta had told them, Tameron looked to be a boy, not an ancient king—courtesy of fae glamor. They usually didn't use it when they were in the fae world among other fae, so Simon was surprised the king would use it.

"These men may turn into fae." Letta motioned to the fae seers. "We can't keep them in the village where Simon and his people live because some of them would want them dead." And then Letta introduced Simon and the others who were with her.

"You have changed." The king was frowning at her, most likely alluding to her new fae aura, realizing she couldn't have a new aura any other way than if she'd been turned.

"Yes, I'm now also a wolf shifter. A brand-new wolf shifter fae accidentally bit me and now I'm one of the Wolf Mountain pack."

"Are you all right with this?" Tameron asked her, frowning.

Simon wondered what the king meant to do to him and his pack members, if Letta said she was unhappy with being a wolf. Or maybe the scorpion king had power so great, he could remove the wolf part of her. Simon hadn't heard of anything like that. Though he reminded himself he hadn't heard of a wolf fae turning a fae before either. He hoped she would want to remain a wolf like them. In fact, he had every intention of convincing her she wanted to stay with him as a wolf, if she had any notion that she didn't want to be one any longer.

"Yes. I'm happy with Simon's wolf pack. I think I can be of service to them."

"You have used your powers on the human fae seers," the king said.

"Yes. I had to. They had taken some of Simon's pack members hostage. I thought of your teachings and suggested we didn't kill these men."

"And now you want me to take them in."

"Yes, if you would. If they went with us to the village, the wolves they had beaten, might turn on them. Or others who might have suffered at the hands of the fae seers."

"Very well. It's good to see you have found a new family to live with." The king was frowning, as though he wasn't entirely happy about what had happened to Letta, or maybe because he felt obligated to take care of the fae seers, when he didn't really want to. "Is the one who bit you also part of the Wolf Mountain pack?"

Simon spoke up then. "No, Your Majesty."

"And when the other wolf wants to find its own people?" the king asked Simon.

"Then she is free to do so." With Simon's blessing! "In fact, I have every intention of helping her in that regard."

The king cast him a sardonic smile. Then he frowned again. "Take good care of Letta. If anything untoward happens to my little princess, you will regret it."

Princess? For real?

Simon bowed his head to the king. He had to mate her. She could be a great help in ruling his wolf pack. She was capable of making quality leadership decisions, was in good stead with the scorpion king, and who knew how that might aid them if their pack needed a powerful fae to help them out sometime in the future. But it was more than that. She had won his people over, all except for Gia and her brothers, and that was an important consideration. And she had completely won him over, and that was the most important consideration.

Letta hugged the king. "We must leave, to ensure some wolves don't try to take over the pack while we're gone."

"I can help to make sure that doesn't happen, if you ever need my aid. You can release the humans now, Letta," the king said, giving her a warm embrace back. "I'm glad you have done well for yourself."

Simon couldn't believe the scorpion king would really offer to help them, though Simon had never considered needing another fae kind to assist him in dealing with the issues arising from his own pack either.

He'd been thinking more in terms of aiding them against other fae.

Letta waved her hand at the five men and they slumped, looking like they were going to collapse. Then they straightened, and they looked afraid now, huddling together, eyes wide, cowering. Good. They needed to show the fae some respect.

Simon took Letta's hand, pulled her into his arms for a hug, and kissed her. He wanted the king to know how much he really meant to protect and care for Letta. But he did wonder if she truly was the king's daughter or not. The king looked like he was younger than her. Simon would not be averse to marrying a princess, though he supposed kissing her could backfire on him if she shoved him away in front of the king.

Her cheeks were rosy, though she kissed him back. Her people were all smiling. Sometimes he could be a little too spontaneous in his actions, but he did want to show that there was more to Letta and him than her just living among them.

"Thank you for taking care of these men," Simon told the king, glad to get them off his hands.

"Thank you for taking care of Letta. We normally don't have visitors or allow it, but in your case, you are welcome to return," the king said to Simon.

"Thank you, Your Majesty. And you are welcome to visit us at any time." Then Simon bowed, and took Letta's hand and they left with the other wolves to return home, minus the human fae seers.

***

Once Simon and the rest of their party had returned to the square in the village, Simon confronted Tomas and his brothers. "Tell us what you had intended to do with us," Simon said to Tomas, his brothers standing on either side of him, the whole pack looking on, having kept the men in the square all this time to stand in judgement.

Gia appeared horrified they might tell the truth. Letta and Myla and her brothers were standing together. The council members were unified also nearby.

Simon had the greatest urge to say that Letta would know if Tomas was telling the truth, but he didn't want his people to fear her.

"We were going to use the fae collars on you," Tomas said honestly.

"And then?" Simon asked. When Tomas failed to answer him quickly enough, Simon said, "To kill us then."

"No. We were going to take you someplace far way and just leave you there."

"And when we returned?" Simon asked.

Tomas glanced at his brothers, both who looked that they were headed for the noose and the hangman's tree and were afraid to say anything to make matters worse.

Tomas let out his breath. "You weren't supposed to return."

"Then you meant to kill us."

"No. You weren't supposed to find your way back

for a good long while."

"Like ever. You thought fae seers would eventually catch up to us. Tomas, you knew if we returned, I'd make you pay for what you did to us. You knew we couldn't return, or we'd tell the pack what you had done to us."

Tomas looked defeated. "We wanted to pay you back for the way Letta treated Gia and you stuck up for the scorpion fae instead of one of our own."

"When one of ours is the one at fault, of course I'll stick up for the one who was not at fault. And Letta is one of ours now. You know I have every right to kill you and your brothers for what you planned to do to us. I don't believe you when you say you just wanted to send us away for a time to make a point. I could very well banish all of you, your sister included, because she knew what you were planning, might have even orchestrated the whole thing and that's why she returned to see how things were going and saw the fae seers taking you hostage. You've always been good pack members, which is the only reason you're not dead now."

Simon glanced at Gia and narrowed his eyes at her. "As to you, Gia, if any of you are involved in anything else that would harm this pack or any of its members, you will be dead. No more allowances."

Then he turned his attention back to the brothers again. "I could have left you to the fae seers who intended to drown you, then it would have been out of my hands. But as your pack leader, it's my duty to deal with your treachery in my own way."

"Spare Remington, if you would," Tomas said. "He tried to talk us out of it."

Simon folded his arms across his chest. "Yet he went with you and he didn't try to stop you at the restaurant. Letta did." Simon paused. "You have lost the ability to fae travel for a year."

Several muffled conversations took place. No one had ever had that happen to them in the pack. He could only imagine what a hardship that would be for the brothers.

"Further, you will be on probation for the entire year. Everything you say and do will be monitored the whole year. If you choose to leave the pack, you can return after a year and Letta will restore your ability to fae travel. Be forewarned, if anything should happen to her during this time and she dies—whether you were instrumental in her death or something else is—you will never be able to fae travel again." He wondered if the king of the scorpion fae could remove the effect, but he wasn't about to mention that here, not sure that he could anyway.

"That's not fair!" Gia shouted.

"If they prefer to die, that's the alternative." Simon wasn't about to change his mind on this issue.

"It's fair," Tomas quickly said, though he didn't look happy in the least about the prospect. But at least he and his brothers were alive and given another chance to do right by them.

His brothers appeared relieved to be allowed to live,

but likewise, they didn't seem happy about the fae travel bit.

The brothers could be real hotheads, and Simon suspected that they hadn't really thought out the plan that well. That it was devised on the spur of the moment in an act of desperation to punish Simon and Letta. It had to have been a last-minute plan because Simon hadn't told anyone, not even Letta, that he was taking her to the restaurant until right before they dressed to leave. Of course, when anyone saw them dressed for the human world and Letta was wearing the little black dress, they could have assumed they were going on a date there.

Simon didn't think there was anything worse that he could have done to them, but take away their ability to fae travel, and let them live with the shame of what they'd tried to do. They'd hate to be watched all year as if they were trouble for the pack, which they now were. He suspected they wouldn't last with the pack, but they might attempt to hold out until they could have their ability to fae travel returned.

Once he had told them what their punishment was in front of the pack, he retired to the cottage with Letta and Myla.

"I can't believe they planned to kill you," Myla said. "And all because of Gia."

"I believe it also has to do with the fact she won't be my mate and they thought their positions would be elevated if she was, so they're furious about Letta messing things up. Not that she has. I would never have taken Gia for my mate, but I'm sure she's convinced them that she was going to be." Simon turned to Letta. "What else can you do with your magic?"

Myla served up chocolate cream pie. Simon set the table.

Letta poured cups of tea for them. "That's a secret. If I need to use my abilities, I will. But for now, it's best to pretend I don't have them. It helps to put my enemies on edge. Now they know of three things I can do: zap them with a charge, take away their transportation, and freeze them. Their imaginations could run wild with speculation. It's like a secret weapon."

"My mind runs wild with speculation," Simon said, as they all took their seats to eat.

Myla smiled. "Mine too. But if it helps Simon to stay in power, and it helps the pack to win its battles, I'm all for it, whatever the power is. While you were gone, the whole pack was talking about what Tomas and his brothers did. They said they knew that Gia was just as much behind the plot. I'm worried your ruling might not be enough."

CHAPTER 13

Ena and Brett met with their staff in the great hall. "Okay," Ena said, "each of you have asked if we would turn into dragons and bite you. Except for Ryker and Jacob. Of course, neither Mark nor Bryan have either. No, we will not shift and bite any of you. What if we seriously injured you and that was the only result? So no. You are all dragon fae and you should be happy and proud of who you are."

"Ena's right," Brett said.

Muriel frowned. "But from what everyone's said, don't you want to even test the theory?"

"No. You know what we do as dragons. What if all the dragon fae were shifters? Then there'd be no one who needed us for special missions."

"Besides," Brett said, "the queen has heard of all this nonsense and has issued an edict that if any dragon bites a fae with the intent to change the fae, both will be banished from the kingdom. It is said she is afraid that all her people will want to be dragons, and she will be the only one in the kingdom who isn't a shifter."

Everyone reluctantly agreed. Even those who hadn't wanted to "test" the theory nodded also.

"Let's get back to work then," Ena said.

Bryan left then to see the queen and Mark returned to the gardens out back, while her maids hurried outside to see to the prized goat and the mischief it was getting into.

Ena was grateful to have Mark working on her water gardens again, while Bryan went to work for the queen to pay off his debt for his short hospital stay. He was honored, but he still preferred being with his friends, Brett and Bryan, and Ena and all her staff. They'd all grown on each other. But she suspected the two men would like to return to the wolf pack now that they were wolf shifters, once they were finished with their jobs at the two castles. They had talked nonstop about all the fun they'd had in fighting with the other wolves.

The prized goat she and Brett had found for a client was now running around their courtyard, eating any plant in plain sight that it could reach. In the beginning, before Bryan and Mark had become her wards, her courtyard had been almost all paving stones, with some shrubs growing at the base of the protective red-stone walls, but after Mark and Bryan had finished creating the gardens out back, they had started on the front. She now had climbing roses growing over trellises, daffodils, daylilies, and several other flowering plants that rivaled the queen's.

The goat was a pretty blond with black boots and a white patch down its nose. Ena had to admit she'd come out to pet it when no one was around to see her do so. But she couldn't abide it eating her plants.

Two of Ena's maids chased the goat off. He might be a prized goat by someone, but he was a real nuisance here, Ena thought.

Ena folded her arms and watched the antics of the women chasing the bleating goat off. Brett joined Ena and slipped his arm around her waist.

"Do you think the man who owned her will pay up?" Brett asked.

"Nope. And it's too late for that now. He said she was being replaced with a new prized goat. I'm giving her as a gift to the queen for helping us with Bryan's hospitalization. It never hurts to do something special to stay in the queen's favor. And I'd rather the goat eat her plants, not mine." Then she smiled. "That didn't sound quite right. The queen loves goats and said she would make the previous owner envious when she entered this goat in the competition and wins."

Brett smiled. "Do you want me to take the goat to her, and then I can check on Bryan's progress in the queen's gardens? I wanted to see how he was doing, as far as whether he is having trouble with shifting or not. I didn't have time to ask earlier."

"Sure. I'm going out back to see how Mark is doing

with our gardens."

Brett kissed her, then shifted, and as a dragon, swooped down, grabbed the startled goat up in his talons and carried her to the queen's castle.

Ena couldn't be gladder that the goat was gone, and her maids could get back to dusting, or whatever they were supposed to be doing. They both looked exhausted, but relieved not to have to be chasing after the goat the rest of the day.

Ena headed for the gardens out back and found Mark and Jacob working on the flow of water for a waterfall. It was just amazing and she was thrilled Mark had returned to finish his work.

"The pond will be filled with koi and the waterfall will help aerate the water. After we have it completely operational, I needed to know if you have any place in this world that has koi?" Mark asked. "I guess I should have asked that first."

"Uh, no. We'll have to transport some here. When will you be ready for them?"

"In a couple of days."

"All right. We'll make a trip to the human world then and pick some up. You're doing a great job."

"Thanks, I love doing this. I never thought I would. I had to mow the grass back home and I hated it."

"I'm glad that you enjoy it here and you have done a miraculous job." Because Ena had really, really needed a gardener. But what Mark and Bryan had done with her gardens was nothing short of a miracle. "How are you feeling, wolf-wise?"

"I'm fine now. I wasn't happy about it at first because of how sick I felt to begin with. And then to be locked up in the cage was humiliating. Having little control over my shifting was exasperating. I always thought it would be cool if Bryan and I could shift like you and Brett into dragons. Of course, I was thinking of dragons or falcons even, not wolves. But I think they're really cool and I like being one."

"Did you meet any she-wolves you really liked in Simon's pack?"

"Yeah, but they didn't like us because we had been fae seers and also because, if we do come into our true fae kind, who knows what we'll be."

"Maybe you'll still get your chance of being a dragon or a falcon. Two fae shifter types then," Ena said, smiling.

"As long as I don't become both at the same time."

Ena could imagine what a mess that would be. A half-furry dragon, or a wolf with dragon wings.

"Hey, after Bryan and I got changed from a bite, I was wondering if a dragon shifter really could change a fae that way. I know everyone's talking about it and I know you don't want to test it out, but I just wondered."

"I've never heard of that happening." Then again, she'd never heard of a dragon biting anyone. They normally just used their flame to deal with problem people or monstrous creatures.

Then she let Mark get back to work. She needed to

locate a place that sold koi, but they had no way of knowing where they could pick up some until they visited the human world. No internet here, and even if they had it, they couldn't connect to the human world. That was an interesting idea though.

She had to thank Simon for returning Mark and Bryan to them also. She hoped Hannah was minding her manners, but Ena was glad she didn't have responsibility for the woman any longer.

Ena didn't have any other mission right now, the other dragons taking care of them so *they* could earn the treasure. She paced for a few minutes around the great hall. Brett would probably be some time while visiting with Bryan, so she decided to just go to Wolf Mountain on her own. She was so used to doing whatever she needed to do without worrying about getting anyone's approval. She was a great dragon shifter and had been unmated all this time. It annoyed her to realize she even had to consider whether or not Brett would approve. It wasn't his business to do so.

Then she took a deep breath. It wasn't so much that he wouldn't approve, she reminded herself, but that he might want to go with her. But waiting around when everyone else in the household was busy wasn't her thing.

She noticed her butler watching her. "Ryker, I'm going to Wolf Mountain." She almost told him why she was going, and then curbed the inclination. She was the head of this household, along with Brett now, and her butler didn't need to know what business she had.

"Does Brett—"

She raised her hand to silence Ryker at once. She wasn't about to allow her staff to question her actions.

"I'll be home shortly. Maybe even before Brett returns. If he does, and I'm still not back, just tell him where I've gone."

Ryker frowned, but inclined his head in agreement.

Then she left the castle, shifted, and flew off as a dragon back to Wolf Mountain. She rarely went there. She couldn't believe she'd be returning again so soon.

When she arrived, she landed in a clearing near the village, then shifted. She trekked to the commons area where there was a squabble going on, and she thought Hannah was causing the trouble. Hannah was standing off to one side, arms folded, headed cocked, smirking, as if she was amused that the wolves weren't getting along. From what Ena could gather, Tomas and his brothers had tried to collar Letta and Simon in the human world and leave them to their fate, or kill them. And several of the wolves there didn't like that Simon was allowing them to live.

Simon's brother, Ronan, saw her and came over to greet her. "Sorry you had to witness the trouble we're having."

"If I can be of any assistance to you and your family, just let me know. I wanted to thank Simon for sending Mark and Bryan back to the dragon fae kingdom."

"He's at the cottage. I'll escort you there. Are either

of them having any trouble with shifting?" Ronan walked her back to the cottage.

"No. They've been doing well. Thanks for asking. How is Hannah?"

"I can see why you don't want her back."

Erin frowned. "That bad, eh?"

"She's staying with Aegis and me. Unlike Mark and Bryan, who were always volunteering to help us with anything that needed to be done, after doing their practice play-fighting and learning to take cues from us about what the different wolf expressions mean. We've been teaching Hannah too, and she's eager to learn about that, but to help out with the ordinary chores? Forget that."

"I can imagine she was probably like that when she was at home in the human world. Speaking of which, she'd better not return there, when the police are probably looking for her as a kidnapped victim, or a possible runaway."

"I'll let her know that. She knows how to transport herself places, but she's sticking close to the village."

"Is she okay with her shifting?" Ena glanced at Ronan.

"Yeah. Better than Mark and Bryan, but I think that's because she was one of us from the beginning."

He knocked at the cottage door and Simon answered it. He smiled brightly when he saw Ena with his brother and she appreciated it. "Are you here to check up on Letta? She is doing great."

"No, actually, I came to thank you for turning Mark and Bryan over to us."

"Come in. Ronan, did you want to have tea with us?" Simon asked.

Myla waved to Ena in greeting.

Ronan shook his head at Simon. "No, thanks. We're still having some issues over your ruling."

Simon raised a brow.

"Some of the wolves believe Tomas and his brothers got off too lightly."

"My decision stands. Just howl for me, if you need me to step in and make my ruling clearer."

"Will do." Ronan waved at Letta and Simon frowned at him.

Ena was amused. It looked like Simon, and maybe his brother, were interested in the scorpion-wolf fae. Ena wouldn't ask if Letta could stay with her any longer. Letta needed to set down roots and it appeared she was happy here where she was.

Ena sat down to have tea with them. She enjoyed the special cookies that Letta and Myla had made, filled with chocolate and mint, and then Ena told them what Mark and Bryan were doing.

"Sounds like they're happy to be home," Simon said. "Though, if they ever need to be around wolves, we'd be happy to give them a home here. Or they can even just come and visit any time they like. We have a great wolf celebration coming up that they need to see."

"I think they liked some of your she-wolves, but the

ladies rejected them for being fae seers before this."

Simon nodded. "Some of our wolves have had issues with the fae seers when they've gone to visit the human world, so it's perfectly understandable. Even Tomas and his brothers ran afoul of them. We did lose three of our pack members to their kind last year. But Mark and Bryan are the same as us now, and they're good people besides. Given time, I'm sure our eligible she-wolves will see them for who they truly are."

"And Hannah?" Ena knew she shouldn't bring her up, in case Simon said he wanted her to take Hannah back with her.

"She's doing as well as can be expected. I'm sure she's giving us no more grief than she gave her parents when she was living at home."

Ena's own parents had been murdered by a previous dragon fae ruler, not one of the shifting kind, and she truly couldn't see how anyone wouldn't love their parents. Then again, maybe Hannah's parents weren't loveable either. They probably weren't her real parents either, not if they were human and she was fae.

A knock on the door sounded, and Simon sighed and headed for the door to open it. "Well, look who's here. A dragon without his armor."

Ena glanced back to see a growly-looking Brett, but as soon as he saw that she was perfectly safe, eating cookies and drinking tea with the other ladies, he smiled. She would have to discuss this business of him being overprotective of her. She was a mighty dragon shifter fae, after all.

CHAPTER 14

Brett smiled at his mate and pulled her in for a hug. Simon was amused to see the dynamics between the two dragon shifters. Ena hugged him back and kissed him, making it appear any problem she had with him being so concerned over her was a thing of the past.

Then Brett sat down with them to have some tea and cookies also. "You would not believe how the rumors are spreading that if a wolf shifter can turn a fae, what if the dragon shifters can? We've had numerous requests from dragon fae who are not shifters for us to turn them."

"That's been a real change from the previous rule," Ena said, "when the dragon shifters had been second-class citizens and only a means to an end. Still, I doubt a dragon's bite could do more than possibly cause an infection, just as anyone's bite could, but it wouldn't turn anyone into a dragon shifter."

Simon and Myla shook their heads.

"No one's tried then?" Myla asked.

"Not that we know of," Ena said. "Certainly, neither Brett nor I will be doing it. Are you going to punish Hannah for what she did to Myla and Letta?"

Simon stretched out his legs. "She had the excuse she was newly turned and didn't have a lot of control over her actions. Just like Mark and Bryan didn't. We kept her locked up for longer, and we'll do it again if we feel she is…unstable."

There was another knock at the door. Simon let out his breath in resignation. "I believe I need to deal with some pack issues. Thanks for dropping by. If I don't see you before you leave, tell Mark and Bryan that they are always welcome here."

"We will," Brett said.

Simon answered the door.

Ronan said, "The rest of our pack needs to hear your ruling again, because some of our members were gone at the time and they don't believe you would let the brothers live after their treachery. One good thing that came out of it—most are stating they wouldn't want them ruling in your place."

"Okay, let's go." Simon left with his brother.

"How are you doing with the pack?" Ena asked Letta.

"I think my abilities can really help them. And I'm enjoying the friendship here. Except, of course, for the issue with Gia and her brothers."

Someone knocked on the door and Myla laughed. "I

swear we never have this much company." She went to the door and smiled. "Come in, Clarita."

Clarita saw the dragon fae shifters and Letta sitting in the living room and she said to Myla, "I didn't mean to interrupt you, but I heard the awful news of how you were attacked. And the she-wolf still lives."

"Your arrival is welcome. We're just visiting. This is Letta, the woman who saved my life. And you know Ena and Brett."

"I've heard about you, Letta. I heard you're a scorpion fae," Clarita said, coming in to join them.

Myla fixed her some tea.

"The same she-wolf who attacked Myla, turned me," Letta said.

Clarita frowned and took the tea cup that Myla offered her. "I didn't think that your kind even existed any longer. And I was surprised a wolf shifter could turn a fae."

"It appears that it can change a scorpion fae. Maybe because my kind have isolated themselves from other fae for so many centuries."

"It surprised us all," Ena said. "Hannah turned two of our humans too. And, I'm sorry to say, we brought the fae seer to our world to begin with. Apparently, she was a wolf shifter all along, who just came of age."

Clarita shook her head. To Letta, she said, "We have our own wolf pack. I don't belong to Simon's. We're winged wolf shifters, if you didn't know."

"I noticed your aura is a sky blue; whereas, the wolf

shifter's aura is more of a woodland green," Letta said.

"Right, for the woods to camouflage them and the blue is for us flying like dragons in the sky." Clarita shifted to show Letta her shimmery wings as a wolf.

Letta smiled. "Beautiful."

Clarita shifted back. "Thank you. We're not opposed to mating wingless wolf shifters, but I think there's just a preference to having a mate who can fly also. It appears you are both okay after Hannah bit you." Clarita smiled at Brett and Ena. "I'm surprised to see you are here."

"We had to drop off the two men who had been turned earlier, though we've managed to bring them home," Brett said. "We wanted to thank Simon for taking them in and teaching them how to be wolves."

Clarita laughed. "I would think that much would come naturally. Then again, I was born a winged wolf shifter. I still think the she-wolf who wreaked so much havoc should be terminated."

"She's being given a chance to live among us and learn how to behave. If not, that's always an option," Myla said.

Another knock sounded on the door.

"We're going to get on our way." Brett squeezed Ena's hand.

She agreed. "Good seeing you, Myla, Letta, and Clarita."

"Likewise," the ladies said.

As they went to the door, Myla opened it to see who was there.

Hannah. She ignored Ena, smiled brightly at Brett, and said to Myla, "Your brother sent me to talk to you."

Ena paused, her dark look directed at Hannah, and Letta suspected she was ready to stay and help deal with her if Myla needed her to.

Myla gave Ena a hug. "Congratulations on your babies again. Letta can visit you any time she wants."

"Thank you." Then Ena and Brett left.

Clarita was eyeing Hannah with contempt.

"I want to know why I was in the human world when I'm supposed to be one of you," Hannah said to Myla.

"Have a seat." But Myla didn't offer her anything to eat or drink.

Hannah took a seat on one of the chairs.

"Princess Alicia was raised there when she is a dragon fae. Though, that's what her mother is. Her father is of the sphinx. And her mother's father, who ruled the dragon fae kingdom, wouldn't let her mother marry her father. They did anyway, then left for the human world so that the king wouldn't kill her father, and maybe the baby. They hid out for years in the human world."

"I wasn't living with fae parents. They were strictly human," Hannah said.

"Not fae seers?" Myla asked.

"No."

"It could be that your parents had taken you there and they died and you were orphaned. No one knew of your whereabouts in the human world so that they could come get you. That's one possibility," Myla said.

"Or, you were so ornery as a child, your fae parents dumped your butt in the human world, figuring it was an easy way to get rid of you," Clarita said.

Hannah frowned at her. "Who are *you*?"

"Your worst nightmare if you hurt Myla again," Clarita said.

Letta immediately liked the winged wolf fae.

"Clarita is my best friend. And Letta is too." Myla smiled at Hannah.

Delighted that Myla included her too, Letta wondered if Hannah had ever had any best friends, even among the fae seers.

"What if I'm like Princess Alicia and have parents of different fae realms? Maybe I'm a princess too." Hannah tilted her chin up, as if to say they would have to treat her like royalty.

Letta was a princess in her own right, though she didn't feel any need to share that bit of news with the wolves. They didn't have titles among them, so it wouldn't make any difference to them.

"That would be a disaster," Clarita said. "I mean about the princess part. Then again, wolves don't have royal designations."

Myla cleared her throat. "And if you are of two different fae, the wolf shifter will be dominant over a regular, non-shifting fae."

"What about a dragon shifter?" Hannah asked.

"We haven't ever seen one of those, so your guess is as good as ours," Myla said. "And we have checked our archives to learn if anyone has left the pack some years ago that we might not remember or were too young to even know about. None of our elders knew about you. None of our wolves are unaccounted for. No one was ready to give birth and then the mother and baby, or just the baby, disappeared either."

"What about other wolf shifter packs?" Hannah asked, looking disappointed.

Unless she changed her attitude, Letta didn't think any wolf pack would want to claim her.

"There are several all over. You might have originally been from one of those," Myla said. "Well, actually, you must have been, since you're not one of ours." Myla sounded glad for that.

Letta didn't blame her.

"I want to look for my wolf pack. There has to be one."

Letta thought Hannah believed the woman would think she'd be better accepted there. Maybe she would, since she hadn't nearly killed anyone in any other wolf packs. Maybe they wouldn't mind her snarky attitude.

"Maybe Tomas or one of his brothers could take you to look for them," Myla said.

Clarita snorted. "They should be dealt with in the same way as her. I heard the news about them too."

"Why did I only just recently become a fae? I mean, if I was born one, how come I only now can do fae stuff? Why not before when I lived in the human world? I just don't understand it," Hannah said.

"Your parents or another fae might have cast a spell on you so that you couldn't turn until you came of age. Not everyone comes of age at the same time. Just like walking and talking for children come at different stages of development for different children, that happens with fae children," Myla said. "And often we don't come into our all our abilities until we're teens. That way we can't skip over to the human world without a guardian and get ourselves in big trouble when we're little."

Simon returned to the cottage and let out his breath. "I don't always make popular decisions for the pack, but, boy, do some of our wolves want blood. Hey, Clarita, glad to see you here."

"I came to see how Letta was doing," Clarita said, then glowered at Hannah, the cause of all the trouble.

"Hannah wants to find her pack. Maybe Tomas or one of his brothers can go with her?" Myla asked Simon.

Letta smiled. She thought it was a great idea.

"Yeah, that would be the way to go. I'll let them know right after we eat."

"I've got to run," Clarita said. "I'm due at Alton's treasure cave for guard duty."

"All right. See you later," Simon said.

Myla gave Clarita a hug and then the winged wolf left the cottage.

"What if Tomas or one of his brothers doesn't want to go with me?" Hannah asked.

"Let me put it this way, he needs to get in my good graces, so if I tell him to go, he's going." Simon opened the door for Hannah. "I'll let you know when you're leaving."

Letta thought he sounded glad to send her on her way. She hoped that Hannah would find her own people. Maybe she'd be happier. Or not. Some people were never happy, no matter where they lived, who they lived with, or what they did with their lives.

"Did you have a nice visit with Clarita?" Simon asked as they began to prepare a boar stew together.

"Yeah, it was. How was your date? Because of Tomas's situation, I didn't get a chance to ask," Myla said.

"It was fun. We actually went to the seacoast."

"Now that sounds good. That's what I need. A guy who will take me to somewhere fun. It's a good thing I wasn't dating Tomas. I had considered it. He was interested, you know, because I'm the pack leader's sister."

"No other reason?" Letta asked, thinking the wolf was a creep, if that's all he wanted. Power through marriage to Myla.

Myla blushed. "I'm sure he liked me too. But that wasn't the ruling factor."

"So how close is the nearest wolf pack from here?" Letta figured it must be a long way away so they wouldn't compete for hunting and fishing.

"About four hours from here. We like to have a lot of territory between wolf packs," Simon said. "We don't really have a lot of problems between packs. We do try to find mates from other packs. We often have pack celebrations as a way of getting to know other wolves."

"The dragon shifters have trials and dragons come from all over to win at competitions. That's their way of finding new dragon mates also," Myla said.

"So what do you do at the wolf gatherings?" Letta asked.

"Feasting, dancing, wolf fights, but also activities like wolf tug-of-war, wolf runs, locating objects of our own as fast as we can," Myla said.

Letta laughed. "Like they do at dog trials in the human world?"

Myla scoffed. "Wolves are not like dogs. But we do have a nose for things, so that's why we do it. We mate for life, unlike dogs."

Letta smiled. It would take some getting used to being a wolf and thinking of doing things in wolf terms.

"So what did you think of Clarita?" Simon asked.

"I love her wings."

"Do you wish you had been changed by one of her kind so you could have wings?" Simon asked.

Myla smiled.

Letta shook her head. "I think it's enough to be a wolf shifter. I'll pass on the wings."

"Are you feeling more comfortable about being a wolf?" Simon asked.

"I'd like to practice some of the things Myla said we'd do at a wolf gathering."

"Dancing?" Myla asked.

"Yes, I don't know how to do that. It's not something our king would have allowed. Not between males and females."

"Simon will have to teach you how to dance."

Someone knocked on the door.

Simon went to the door and Letta was surprised to see it was Tomas. "Yeah, Tomas?"

"Hannah came by my cottage and said you wanted me to take her to find her wolf pack."

"Yeah. I think she'd be happier with her own people."

"Or not," Tomas said. "I didn't think she had a pleasant bone in her body, but she seemed to perk up when you told her she could go looking for her pack."

"I just hope you can find her pack."

"And she's happy with it."

"Thanks for taking her with you to find them."

"We'll be back for the wolf celebration in three days. If we don't find them before that, maybe one of the wolves from one of the packs attending the celebration will know Hannah is one of theirs."

"All right. When will you leave?"

"First thing in the morning."

"Okay, safe travels." Simon hoped she wouldn't be coming back, and he wondered if Tomas was feeling so much heat from his earlier actions that he wanted to leave for a while. He might even want to see about leaving their pack for another, but once news traveled to other packs about what Tomas and his brothers had pulled, the other packs might be unwilling to take them in.

CHAPTER 15

The next day, Ena considered the beauty of the waterfall cascading into the pool below and how it wound around the gardens with little stepping stones or bridges traversing it. She was envisioning the fish swimming in the water and found Mark looking over the rose garden.

"Are you ready to find some koi and bring them here?" Ena asked Mark.

"Yeah, absolutely."

Jacob hurried to join them. "Can I go too?"

Once Jacob had joined her staff, he'd been kind of lost with not knowing what to do as far as a job went, yet he wasn't one to sit idle. He'd needed work to earn enough money to save to provide for a family, though he hadn't found a wife yet and he hadn't wanted to leave Ena and Brett's employ. Once he began helping Mark and Bryan in the gardens, he'd found his new job and he would take over when Mark left to join the wolf pack.

"Sure, you can go with us, Jacob," Ena said, smiling. She'd never regretted taking him into her family. She only wished Bryan could go with them on this adventure. She knew he'd appreciate what they were doing. Not to mention that the queen would want koi in her gardens next. Still, Ena wanted them in *hers* first.

When the three of them arrived at a strip mall in Dallas, Texas, in their invisible forms, she watched people coming and going. Then she saw what she wanted to grab. A man had just finished texting on his cell phone. When he pocketed it, she hurried to follow him to his car, slipping her hand in his pocket, and pulling his phone out. She whipped around, turned visible, and hoped he hadn't noticed her stealing his phone.

Mark and Jacob had turned visible and were watching her, smiling. The man got into his car and backed out of the parking space while Ena handed the phone to Mark. She didn't know how to access the phone since she'd never lived in the human world. She only knew what they were used for.

Mark looked eager to have a phone in his hand again, after having lost his own that wouldn't work in the fae world. He did a search for koi shops while Ena and Jacob looked over his shoulders.

"That is amazing." Jacob had rarely been to the human world before Mark and Bryan had ended up living with them, so it appeared he hadn't seen a phone up close.

"This pet shop." Ena pointed to the one that was closest to their location, at least according to the listings for shops selling koi.

Mark sighed. "Man, what I wouldn't do to have a phone again."

Ena folded her arms. "Yeah, but it wouldn't work in our world. You realize you really are part of our world now."

"Yeah, not that I wanted to ever return here for good. It's been such an adventure in your world. And now having your fae abilities and being a wolf shifter life couldn't be better."

"It's your world too now."

Looking pleased, Mark smiled.

The way Jacob was eyeing the phone, Ena swore he wouldn't mind having one too! "Look how antisocial everyone is." She couldn't imagine being with her friends or others and ignoring them to stare down at a little device all day.

They glanced in the direction she was looking. It was a café where people were sitting, eating with others, but everyone was on a phone, tapping away, or swiping a finger across the phone's screen.

"If you had one that could do all that a phone could do, you'd be on it too. Just think, you wouldn't have to return to the quest board to see what had been posted that needs to be taken care of: missing goats, rings, people. You could look on the internet and easily find quests from all over the fae territories. Not just from your region," Mark said.

She scoffed. "That's not what they are using the phones for. Not for work." She turned invisible and walked over to the café and peered at the phones people were using. "Games. Love texts." Though that part she wouldn't mind. She could text Brett to let him know where she was and...well, the love stuff she wouldn't want to share over a phone. That had to be done in person.

The couple at the table where she was looking over their phone messages glanced around, trying to see where her voice had come from.

Mark was smiling. She knew he would never get used to seeing the fae at work, only now he saw her as visible instead of just seeing her fae aura around an invisible fae, and he was himself invisible. She could tell he thought that was pretty cool.

Mark began looking over someone else's text and swiping his finger across the screen. No one could see that he was there, and when his finger swiped across the man's, the guy's fingers would become numb. Ena and Jacob joined Mark to see what he was doing.

The man kept trying to type something and Mark kept changing the letters on him.

"Damn autocorrect," the man grumbled and pocketed his phone.

Mark laughed and the man glanced around to see who was laughing at him.

Ena strolled off and Mark and Jacob followed her.

"Okay, now that we've had some fun, we need to do what we came here to do." She normally wasn't one to waste her time playing with the humans. She didn't get paid any treasure to do so, and as a dragon, that was her sole purpose in life. To collect as much as she could. Except for being with Brett, she had to admit. And now she was going to have twins and she knew her priorities would change once again. Still, the fae were born with an innate need to play mischief, and she had to admit she'd have fun with Mark and Jacob over the phone business.

When they arrived at the shop carrying the koi, she lost Jacob, who had to get into the pen to play with a bunch of puppies. She shook her head, but he loved taking care of the horses back home, and he seemed to have a real affinity for animals.

She and Mark continued walking to the area where the fish tanks were on display.

Mark was again on the phone and she looked down to see what he was doing. He was reading all about koi. Okay, now that was related to work and since they didn't have koi back home, she could see how important it was to learn how to care for them.

"My foster parents had a koi pond and I used to care for them. So I know something about it. But this is important." He showed her an article about selecting the healthiest fish.

"Oh, good to know, Mark. I never really thought of that part of the equation."

Mark asked a clerk to help them, and they selected

five of the koi. The clerk bagged them up for them.

"Let's get Jacob." Ena led Mark to where Jacob was holding a sleeping puppy. "Do you want to stay here and play with the puppies longer?" She really didn't want to leave him alone in case fae seers showed up. She knew he didn't want to give up the puppy. She sighed and relented. "Do you want the puppy?"

He smiled at her so brilliantly, she didn't have the heart to say no. She knew everyone at the castle would fall in love with the adorable puppy, though she reminded herself she was a fierce dragon warrior and having a brand-new puppy under foot wasn't something she would normally agree to. But everything had changed when Brett came into her life.

"You'll need a dog bed," Mark said.

"We can make one," Ena said frowning.

"Dog food."

"We can make our own. Cook may not be happy about it though." But Ena suspected she would be thrilled.

"Dog dishes. A dog leash. Collar. Chew toys." Mark handed her the bag of koi and hurried off down the aisle featuring dog merchandise so he could get the other items. Price wasn't an issue because they just took what they needed and...vanished.

"All right, Jacob, you can keep the puppy." As if she felt she had any say in it now. She could just see Mark with all the dog supplies and her telling him he had to put them all back. She ended up carrying the fish while

Mark had his hands full of dog stuff, including a bed because he said they couldn't make one fast enough for the puppy, and Jacob, carrying the puppy, transported to their world. She was thrilled her fish pond would be complete. She wasn't sure about taking care of a new puppy. Not that she'd be the one responsible for it. She suspected everyone on her staff would pitch in to take it out for potty breaks and clean up messes it accidentally made.

When they arrived in the gardens, Mark said, "You know the queen will want a koi pond too as soon as she learns you have one."

"At least you know where you can find some koi now. If she wants some, just let me know, and I'll go with you. I don't want you going alone." Ena carefully released the fish into the new pond.

"Yeah, sure. I'm going to teach Jacob how to take care of the fish, and Muriel wanted to help too. That way when I'm living with the wolves, the koi should thrive."

"Okay, good, that sounds perfect."

Brett came out to join them. He raised a brow at the sight of the puppy, and at all the dog items Mark was still holding. "Did you get any fish?"

"Very funny," Ena said. "We read up on them before we picked out the ones we brought home, healthy, not just pretty colors, but they were some of the prettiest ones." She turned to Mark. "You and Bryan are going to the Gathering of the wolf packs, right?"

"Yeah," Bryan said, suddenly appearing in the

gardens. "I had to see what Mark and Jacob did with the gar—woah... love the koi. Where did you get them?"

"Your former world. I suspect we'll have to make another trip there for the queen's water gardens, if she hears about them and wants some too, but for now, we need to feed you so you can return to the wolf pack before the Gathering begins," Ena said.

Muriel came out to see the fish but she grinned at the puppy and wanted to hold him. "Oh, how adorable. You only brought one home? He will be so lonely. He needs a litter mate."

"We'll be his litter mates," Ena said, frowning.

Brett smiled at her.

Right. Saying she was going to be a litter mate to a puppy didn't sound dragon-like at all. "You know what I mean."

Muriel looked crestfallen.

"All right, all right. One more puppy. No more than that. Just one." Sheesh, Ena was going to have to work on her I'm-a-dangerous-dragon, hear-me-roar-and-take-heed role.

"I'll help you," Mark said. "We'll need more dog supplies."

"I'll go with you too so we can find just the right puppy for you," Jacob said.

"You can't take the puppy back there." Ena could see them getting caught with it.

Mark handed Brett the supplies and Jacob held out the puppy to Ena. Everyone, including her mate, waited to see what she would do. Letting out her breath, she took hold of the puppy and it licked her chin.

She couldn't help loving it. The puppy was adorable. She cuddled it and headed for the castle.

"I'm going too," Bryan said.

Ena called out over her shoulder, "Just *one* more puppy."

"Are you sure the four of you will be all right without us?" Brett asked Mark and the others.

"Piece of cake," Mark said.

Then he and the others transported back to Dallas as Ena went inside the castle and Brett followed behind her with all the dog supplies. Everyone was excited to see the puppy, but Ena didn't give her charge over to any of her staff. Even Ryker came to see the puppy and smiled.

"Someone will have to housebreak the puppy," Ryker said.

"Yes, everyone who sees that the puppy needs to go out, will have to rush" –Ena held up the puppy so she could see what sex it was—"him out."

It didn't take long before Mark had returned with more dog supplies, Muriel had another puppy that looked like the other, and even Jacob had picked up more dog supplies.

"Where's Bryan?" Ena asked, worried that he hadn't returned with the others.

"We helped him pick out some more healthy koi and he's taken them to the queen's gardens. He said she would make him go get them when she learned you had them in your garden." Mark handed off an armful of dog supplies to Cook. "I'm going over there to teach some of her staff how to take care of the koi and then Bryan and I'll be back to eat before we return to the wolf pack."

"What are the puppies' names?" Ryker asked.

"Duke for the male," Jacob said.

"And Duchess for the female," Muriel said, "because they're part of a royal dragon family."

"Wait, the other is a female?" Ena should have said to get two of the same sex. No way did she want to have oodles of puppies.

Jacob and Muriel smiled. All fae were devious and they'd just pulled a good one on Ena.

"Figure out where they'll sleep, where they'll eat, and be sure they're housebroken quickly."

It didn't seem to matter what jobs her people were supposed to be doing. Everyone wanted a say about where the puppies went to sleep.

When Mark and Bryan returned to eat with them a couple of hours later, Bryan said, "You wouldn't believe how happy the koi made the queen. She was ready to give us both knighthoods."

"We were careful not to mention the puppies though or we were afraid she'd want some too," Mark said.

"Good." Ena was glad for that much anyway.

After that, they all went in to eat the nooning meal.

"They're little dogs, right?" Ena asked, as they sat down to eat at the dining table.

"St. Bernards," Jacob said. "You don't want a dog

that's so small everyone would be stepping on it."

"Or so little that it would get lost in the big castle," Mark said.

"Well, before they get to be big dogs, be sure to housebreak them."

Brett smiled at Ena and she had to admit, despite not wanting to, the puppies were fun. Until there were squabbles about which room the puppies would sleep in. Then everyone, but Ena and Brett, were drawing straws about which puppy would sleep in the staff members' rooms on which night.

CHAPTER 16

Later that day at the Wolf Mountain pack village, Letta left the cottage to get some potatoes. Every time she walked outside, she felt she was on guard constantly while Gia and her brothers were still in the pack. Though she suspected none of them would try anything while the brothers were unable to transport anywhere on their own. She dug up some potatoes from the garden and brought them in to Myla, who was preparing lunch for them.

Letta was excited about the upcoming wolf gathering where pack members would be in several different competitions—matching speed, stealth, and prowess in hunting, strength games, and teamwork. Even food competitions were being held. That's what Myla wanted to participate in. Letta was going to help her, but she really wanted to do some of the other activities. She wasn't really ready for competing as a wolf with others though.

And no one would be there to compete with Letta if she used her magic skills. Three winged wolf packs were there that had teams in the winged wolf competitions. She wanted to watch them, well, and a bunch of other activities also.

Days of preparations had begun, people preparing food and those participating in the games were practicing for the games. Letta would just be an observer so she could see what it was they all did. Every day as wolves, Simon ran with her in the woods as a way of courting her, and took her to the dragon village to eat at a pub, and other restaurants in the human world, even taking in a couple of movies. But the next day the festivities were to begin.

The most beautiful music had been playing all morning as wolves practiced for the competitions. It was as if the goddesses above had turned the whole village into a symphony of seasons and sunrises and sunsets, the most awe-inspiring musical combinations that made her want to sprout wings and fly high above.

"Enchanting, isn't it?" Myla asked. "I always feel I can do twice as much work when they play their music for days on end."

"It's beautiful. I can create music, but only through my magic."

"Really?" Myla began to cut up the potatoes and Letta helped her.

"Like the Pied Piper, drawing people to me, or like the fae of old who made people dance forever."

"Oh, so it's more of a way to conquer your enemies, to control them."

"Or to make your friends fear nothing as you lead them into battle."

"But wouldn't it affect all fae in the vicinity?"

Letta shook her head and put the potatoes into the skillet. "I can target certain fae, and everyone else will just enjoy the music."

"Can you do it without targeting any fae?"

"I can, but I'm still using my magic to do it."

"Can you put a fae to sleep with your music."

"Yes, that too."

"Wow. Play some music while we make the meal."

"I can just see your brother banning my use of magic."

Simon entered the cottage. "What am I missing?" He had to have overheard some of their conversation.

Myla smiled. "She can make her own music. I command you to play it so we would enjoy making the meal."

Letta motioned to the window. "If I play my music, we won't be able to hear the fascinating sounds out there."

"Oh, come on, you have me intrigued," Myla told Letta.

"They will stop playing their own," Letta warned.

"Then you will be influencing them?"

"Not through my use of magic. They will be as captivated as you to see who is playing it. And really, it will be cheating."

"Did you have to learn how to use magic to create the music?" Simon asked and he sounded so much like his sister.

"Every bit of it, yes."

"Okay, so they had to learn how to create their music with their instruments and their voices. It's the same difference. It might just seem to you like it's cheating, but for one who has no musical talent whatsoever, I applaud you. Well, I would, but I need to hear your music first."

"All right, and if I get into trouble for this, I told you so." Letta really didn't want to stop the others from playing their music, because she was enjoying it so much, but she knew that as soon as she played, everyone would quit to hear hers.

Most of the packs had already gathered in the Wolf Mountain territory and set up camps throughout the woods. Some of the pack leaders would stay with Simon and his brothers. Letta wondered if she needed to take a room somewhere else because of it. Hannah was being moved to another household, if she returned with Tomas, so that Ronan and Aegis could take in a pack leader and his sister.

Letta pulled out a flute and began to play her music. The melodies outside continued to play for a while, but one after another of the wolves' songs faded away, and her tune was the only melody that could be heard all around the territory, so hauntingly beautiful that Myla almost burned the lunch.

"Oh my goddess, don't quit playing, just keep going." Myla quickly dished out the meal. "Forget it. It's time to eat. You can play for us after we eat."

Letta smiled at her. She was fun to be with and though Simon was in charge of the pack, Myla often told him what he should do. He never seemed to mind, sometimes taking her advice, sometimes not.

Someone knocked on the door, and Simon let out his breath in exasperation. "Everyone knows I'm at the nooning meal." He left his chair and answered the door. "Ronan. What is going on? I'm eating."

"We want to hear more of the music coming from here. Was it Letta?"

"Yes, and she's eating too."

"Is she using magic?"

"Yes. Go away until we've finished eating. I'm sure she'll play a little more, but I'm sure she doesn't want to stop everyone else from playing their tunes."

"All right. I'll let everyone know that she'll play for us again after the meal. And I came to tell you Hannah is back. She's staying with Gia, who is not happy about it at all, but she shouldn't have been in the plot against you then. Anyway, Hannah didn't find a pack that would acknowledge that she belonged to them."

"But they could have been her pack and they didn't want her joining them?" Simon asked.

"Possibly. She acted so annoyed about no one wanting her to join them, and you know how wolves are—wary, watching every nuance of her actions. Tomas wasn't happy that he had to return with her either. She complained he shifted and ran and tried to lose her in the woods."

"All right, well, maybe someone who shows up at the Gathering will know of her and claim her for their pack. Even if we're stuck with her, she'll have a pack to live with, unless she doesn't do her part." Simon paused and frowned at his brother. "My food is getting cold."

"Hannah is annoyed that everyone took Letta in and even the leader is interested in her for his mate," Ronan said.

Letta scoffed. "I'm from a warrior race of fae that killed off many of our own kind, yet we worked hard to maintain our way of life. No matter which way she goes, she will have to live with herself and what she wants to accomplish or doesn't. She needs to be more helpful and make an effort to be more pleasant around others. Smile a little. I'm sure she doesn't want to return to live in the human world among the fae seers, who would want her death. But maybe she'd prefer that."

Despite that Hannah had attacked and turned her, Letta had tried to be pleasant enough to her, but it didn't seem like Hannah wanted to change her attitude so Letta finally told Ronan, Simon, and Myla what she thought of her.

"She thinks you believe you are better than her," Ronan said.

"I think I'm nicer than her and if that makes me

better than her, then yes, I am." Letta smiled at Ronan.

He smiled back at her in a way that said he was still interested in courting her if things didn't work out between her and Simon. She'd never seen him smile at Hannah, but then what was the use? Everyone knew a smile or a greeting would be met with a sour face or a non-response. So why make the effort to be friendly to the woman? No one mistreated her. They had just learned to ignore her like she wasn't even there.

Ronan said to Letta, "I can't wait to hear your music again."

"I'm almost done eating. I'll play while Myla and I are cleaning up."

Still smiling, Ronan inclined his head to her, then left.

Simon shook his head and shut the door. "He knows not to interrupt me when I'm eating my meal unless it's an emergency I need to deal with." He sat down to eat. "So does your music compel the listener to listen?"

"No, not through the use of magic but apparently it still has that affect. I was enjoying listening to the others playing their music though."

They finally finished their meal and Myla carried her plate into the kitchen. "Letta, I really, really want you to watch everything that's going on at the Gathering. It's the only way you'll be able to learn what's available to do and then next year, maybe you can train so that you can participate if you'd like."

"But I was going to help you with meal

preparations." Letta carried her dish and Simon's to the kitchen.

"You can do that any time. I want you to just enjoy yourself for your first ever wolf Gathering. We hope Bryan and Mark will be here for it too."

Simon took a drink of his tea and agreed. "You need to see all that is offered. But I think you need to enter the music competitions. There are several categories: vocal, instrumental, otherworldly, group, solo."

"Magical?" Letta knew he was forgetting that part.

"She had to learn how to create her own songs and how to use the magic, but she still believes it's cheating," Myla said.

"Nonsense. The ones who play their music had to learn to use their instruments, create their own songs, and train their voices, if they sing, like I said. That's the same as you, but different," Simon said.

"If I win—"

"You win," Simon said. "If you move the rest of the listeners with your music the way you moved me—"

"And me," Myla said.

"I'd venture to guess that you'd win."

Letta heard Mark talking to someone near the cottage, and she peeked out the window to see him and Bryan headed up the walk to the door. "They're here!" She felt a kinship to them for having been turned by the same wolf and locked in cages for a time in the same hut.

Letta opened the door before they could knock and smiled. "I'm so glad you're here! I mean, all of us are glad."

"We heard this beautiful music, and Ronan said we couldn't go near the cottage until you were finished eating. We heard the dishes being set on the kitchen counter and figured you were done," Mark said.

"Come in," Simon said.

"Yeah, you should have seen everyone gathered about outside, waiting to hear the music again," Bryan said. "Who was playing?"

"Our very own Letta," Simon said.

"Don't let the dragon fae queen hear her play or she'll want her to become part of her royal staff," Bryan said.

"That's for sure. Are you joining us for good?" Simon asked.

"Yeah. We're done with our jobs, but if they want us to return to plan some more gardens, they'll pay us. If you're agreeable, we want to live among you," Mark said.

"That's great news! Did you want to eat?" Myla asked. "We've finished, but we have enough for you also."

"Oh, no, thanks. We ate in the dragon fae territory before we came here. They wouldn't have it said that they sent a couple of hungry wolves back to the pack without their nooning meal," Bryan said.

"We're thrilled to have you back for good." Myla finished cleaning the dishes.

Simon and Letta agreed with Myla.

"A problem might be brewing, though," Mark said.

"Not with us, but with Letta."

"Oh?" Simon asked.

"Yeah. The word has gotten around about the woman who is a scorpion fae with magical powers. And that she was the one who removed Tomas and his brothers' ability to transport as the fae," Bryan said.

"And that she was the one making the music because no one in the pack had heard it before. They thought she was just a scorpion fae, but then someone said that she'd been turned, and they wanted to know who had turned her," Mark said.

They all sat down to drink tea in the living room, and Letta thought the men made great spies.

"Don't tell me," Simon said, his voice dark with annoyance. "Someone told them that Hannah turned her, and she's looking for her own pack."

"Yeah," Mark said. "How did you know?"

"I guessed."

"Yeah, and they intend to claim that both Hannah and Letta are their pack members then," Bryan warned.

"Hannah is free to go anywhere she pleases," Simon said.

Letta smiled at him.

Simon cleared his throat and wrapped his arm around Letta. "Letta is staying with me. As my mate."

Letta closed her gaping mouth. "Aren't you supposed to ask me this first?"

Myla punched her brother in the shoulder. "Yes. He is. Do it right, Simon, or she may just walk out of here and join another pack." She sounded extremely irritated with her brother, even if he was the pack leader.

"Of course, that's what I meant. Letta will mate me." Simon raised his brows and smiled at her. "Won't you?"

Letta laughed. She'd thought about his proposing to her since they'd been courting, wondering when it would happen, figuring it wouldn't be long. She certainly never expected the offhanded way he did it. She thought a romantic dinner somewhere, candle lights, music playing, good food and drink would make for a nice ambience when he proposed. And if he hadn't done so soon, she was proposing to him. She never thought that he would propose solely to her because he was trying to claim her before another pack did. What a strange turn of events.

"You notice she hasn't said yes yet," Mark said. "Maybe she'd be my mate."

Bryan laughed at him. "No way. If I were her, I'd definitely stick with the pack leader."

Myla folded her arms. "The Gathering hasn't started yet. Take her to South Padre Island for an ice cream cone, or better yet, a triple hot fudge sundae."

Simon was smiling when he rose from the sofa and offered his hand to Letta. "Want to go to the beach?"

Letta smiled and took ahold of his hand.

"See you later. Tell everyone who is waiting to hear her play her music, they will have to wait until we return." Then Simon swept her into his arms, kissed her, and transported her to the human world.

She loved how Simon could screw up a proposal, his sister could make a recommendation to do better, and he was happy to take her up on her suggestion!

CHAPTER 17

Simon and Letta appeared on the beach near the ice cream shop in South Padre Island, startling a couple of seagulls that quickly flew off.

"What are you going to do when we return to the village if some of the wolves are angry that I agreed to mate you?" Letta asked Simon as they walked into the ice cream shop and she ordered a triple hot fudge sundae with a scoop of coffee ice cream, chocolate, and mint chocolate chip.

He picked out a large chocolate milkshake.

Simon was so glad he brought Letta here because this definitely had the effect he was going for, convincing her to be his. "You want to mate me?"

They took their seats outside on the veranda, the big blue and white striped umbrella keeping the sun off them while they watched the humans playing in the surf, walking along the beach, building sandcastles, or lying out to roast their skin.

Four more couples were sitting out on the deck near them, enjoying ice cream treats.

She sighed and slipped her spoon into her ice cream again. "It's inevitable. Don't you think?"

"No. I never thought it was inevitable. I thought I'd have to earn your favor. I don't know what came over me to propose to you in the way in which I did."

"You were desperate."

He laughed.

She smiled. "You were. Here all these men would be proposing marriage to me and you would have to try and convince me that you were the only one for me."

"I would do anything to convince you of that."

She reached over and took his hand and squeezed, then released him. "I wouldn't want to be with anyone else. Don't you feel the strong pull? Scorpion fae have an ability to 'see' the one who seems to be right for them, though I had to overcome my annoyance with you for sticking me in a cage."

He chuckled. "For your own good. Wolves experience the same thing." He gave a heavy sigh of relief, leaned over, and kissed her. "You've made me the happiest wolf alive."

"You've made me happy too. When I set out on my journey, I had no idea if anyone would even want to be with a scorpion fae. Even though I am a princess."

"Well, so you are a princess."

"The king is my grandfather. So now what do we

do?"

"The Gathering celebration doesn't start until tomorrow. We'll have our mating celebration upon our return. That way everyone who is at the Gathering will know for sure that you aren't available and you're not joining another pack. But if you want more time to prepare, we can wait."

"I don't need any more time. Gia needs to know she has no chance with you."

"She had to have figured that out after she tried to kill you." He finished his milkshake. "Good, then it's settled."

Once Letta finished her ice cream, they walked along the beach, shoes in hand, toes digging into the sand.

"Do you want to go swimming?" Simon thought it could be fun. It was nice and warm out. "We could go to one of the beach shops to grab what we need."

"Sure. Let's do that." Letta and Simon headed through the sand to the shops.

They saw royal guards of the dark fae walking next to the shops, invisible to humans. Simon waved to them. "They come here to ensure that other fae don't try to take over their human territory."

"But they're dark fae when you're a wolf."

"We're friends with the dragon fae, and through Princess Alicia's marriage to the dark fae crown prince, we are friends of theirs."

"We took them in for a time, though the dark fae

royal guard were searching for them so they may not see me in a good way."

"You are a wolf fae like me."

He had his hand on the door of a shop that sold swimwear, beach towels, T-shirts, and more when she said, "You know, we probably need to see my brother in the human world at the home where I spent many years. Would you like to?"

"Do your parents still live there?" He was surprised she'd all of a sudden mention a brother.

"No, but my brother does. We should see him. Come, let's go."

Simon was pondering if she felt her brother needed to approve of their mating first. He wondered how her brother would feel about how she had been turned. Simon hoped he wouldn't try to change Letta's mind about him. "All right. Let's go."

When they finally arrived at a redwood cabin surrounded by a deck in the Ozark Mountains, the pine tree scents gave Simon the urge to run as a wolf. "Could we run out here?" They climbed the steps to the front deck.

"Sure. I never thought I'd be running through the woods where I used to play as a girl, except as a wolf now. We can do that after you meet my brother, Griffin." She knocked on the door and a man, who had the same long, pale-blond hair and blue eyes, opened the door and looked from her to Simon. It was more a look of speculation, than appearing to be glad to see his sister or the stranger on his doorstep.

"You are hanging out with wolves now, dear sister." He opened the door wider to allow them entrance and then turned and headed to the kitchen.

She and Simon entered the cabin and Simon shut the door.

"Sodas? Water? Tea?" Griffin asked.

"Griffin, this is Simon, who has taken me into his wolf pack."

"Tameron kicked you out then." Griffin brought them bottles of water, not waiting for them to tell him what they wanted.

"It was time. I wanted a mate and I found Simon. I'm a wolf too now." She raised her hand as soon as her brother's head swung around to glower at Simon. "He didn't do it. A fae seer, who was taken in by the dragon shifter fae, turned, and attacked me and Simon's sister. Anyway, I took care of Myla's injuries, and Simon offered me a home."

"It sounds to me like he's offered more than that."

"To be his mate, yes. He's the pack leader of the Wolf Mountain pack."

"You could join us if you'd like," Simon offered. Not that he really wanted a non-wolf in the pack, but if it made Letta happy, he was willing to do whatever it took.

"He must not know of our pledge," Griffin said, then took a drink of his water. "We aren't to congregate or if we do, we could become warlike with our kind all over again. King Tameron only has the young ones under his tutelage. Once they grow old enough, they must find their way to other fae kingdoms and became productive and dutiful citizens of the other fae realms. Some of us live in the human world. Like me. But a wolf?" Griffin shook his head. "I didn't think wolf shifters could turn fae kind. I hope the wolf is past tense."

"It is so good to see you, my brother," Letta said, changing the subject.

"How is our old grandfather?"

"Looking as young as ever. We dropped some fae seers off with him to deal with."

Griffin laughed. "To practice what he preaches."

"Do you live here always?" Simon knew some fae loved to live in the human world, despite the danger of running into the fae seers. The fae lived for danger. It was just part of their nature.

"I love living out here with nature. Sure, I could live at home in the world of fae and try to make a go of it somewhere. But I like creating trouble for the humans." Griffin shrugged. "I have a bowling alley I love to go to. My favorite pastime is messing up the champion's game. You should see the looks on everyone's faces as they watch that ball take a little detour into the gutter."

Simon didn't bother going to the human world to play pranks on the humans. He'd always been too busy being groomed to be a pack leader with all the responsibilities that came with the job. It wasn't that he didn't have the inborn trait to mess with the humans, he just didn't have the time.

"I can see Simon's disapproving look. He's a responsible pack leader. He will be way too dull for you, sister." Then Griffin smiled. "Come on. It is time for the bowling games to start. Let's have some fun. Shall we?"

Simon wanted to run as a wolf with Letta. He hadn't intended to prove to Letta's brother that he could enjoy being a typical fae where the humans were concerned, but he went along with it. "All right. A couple of games and then Letta and I are going for a wolf run."

They transported to the bowling alley then, where the lights were tuned off and black lights were on. Then LED disco lights and multi-colored lane lights came on.

"Isn't this great?" Griffin asked. "I love glow bowling."

Letta laughed. "This is great."

Simon had to agree.

Neon-colored balls were rolling down the lanes to knock down neon-colored pins. Many of the people were dressed in either fluorescent clothes or white clothes, which made them glow. The fae weren't there to glow. Simon, Letta, and Griffin were invisible to the humans as they watched the neon balls rolling down the lanes.

"You, first," Griffin said to Simon, as if he were the guest of honor in starting the fae games with the bowlers.

Simon didn't believe humans losing a bowling game was any big deal. Games like these didn't mean anything to him. A tug-of-war contest between wolves, now that proved real teamwork, and strength, and competitiveness.

Simon transported to the middle of one of the lanes and as soon as the ball rolled toward him, he hit it with the side of his foot, knocking it into the gutter. He hadn't thought he'd feel any real pleasure in messing up the guy's game, but the astonished looks on everyone's faces did amuse him. He was fae, after all. He bowed to Griffin and then transported back to where he and Letta were standing.

Griffin motioned for Letta to have a go at it, but she shook her head. Her brother went to another lane and waited right near the pins. Then he knocked the ball into the gutter before it reached its target.

"I told you this place is haunted," the bowler said.

"I keep thinking something's wrong with the balls or the lane but the next time we play, they're fine," another man said.

"Yeah, which makes me think they're haunted. This place, I mean."

"We should go to the other bowling alley."

"I go there too," Griffin told Simon. "I wouldn't want the owner to lose all his business here. What fun would there be in that? I don't mess with the beginners. They have a hard-enough time trying to hit anything. No little kids either. Even if they're really good. I just go after the overconfident guys. I'm headed to the movies. Good to see you, Letta." He gave her a hug. And then he shook Simon's hand. "Treat her well or you'll be hearing from me." Then he vanished.

"Scorpion fae. He has to show how tough he is. Are you ready for the run?" Letta asked, sounding relieved that they were finished here and her brother seemed to approve of Simon.

"Yeah. And then we can return home so we can tell the pack we're mating. I'm sure everyone's eager to hear you play your music too. I know I am."

They walked through a couple people in the bowling alley standing in their path. That was one of the things he liked about being a fae. If humans got into their way, he didn't have to wait for them to move, he could just walk straight through them. The two women shivered.

"I felt so numb all of a sudden," the one said.

"Yeah. And it's happened to me before when I've been here."

Simon smiled and took Letta's hand and transported her to the woods.

They shifted and began running through the predominantly evergreen forest. He loved being here with her like this in a new wilderness. They ran for a good hour when they heard a couple of wolves howl, his brother Aegis, and his council member Steel. Simon howled back and turned to head in their direction. He wondered what was wrong now. No one would have come after him if they hadn't had trouble back at the pack. He thought about humans who might hear the haunting sounds of the wolves in the area when he didn't think any real wolves lived out in these woods.

When they reached the wolves, he greeted them.

They all shifted. "What's wrong?" Simon asked.

"There's fighting among two wolf packs who are there for the Gathering. The leaders both claim that Hannah is theirs and they want to lay claim to Letta because she was bitten by one of their own," Aegis said.

"Oh, really. When only one pack could truly claim the woman. Since that's never been an issue that we've heard of, I wonder where they got that idea." Simon put his arm around Letta's shoulders. "What about Mark and Bryan? Do they want them too?" He figured they wouldn't.

"Nope. They just want Letta and they'll put up with having Hannah," Aegis said, smiling.

"All right. We're done here. It must have taken you some time to find us."

"Yeah, we followed your dust trail to the beach in South Padre Island, then to the cabin near here, then we finally assumed you were off running in the woods and we were trying to catch up to you. I figured we needed to just howl to get your attention."

That did the trick.

"All right, let's go." But Simon was thinking he needed to keep Letta under lock and key or someone was sure to attempt to steal her away from him.

"It's her scorpion fae magic I think they're the most interested in," Aegis said.

"Her singing," Steel said. "And that she's a healer."

Letta folded her arms and raised a brow. "Not for my beauty, kindness, and intelligence?"

"That's why I love you." Simon kissed her and then returned her to their world and to the village.

When they arrived, Simon could see how serious the altercations were. The two pack leaders had shifted and were tearing into each other as wolves. He couldn't believe it. Especially since neither of them had a chance to take Letta home with them. He suspected Hannah didn't belong with the packs either.

"A little early for the wolf competitions, isn't it? They start tomorrow," Simon said.

The wolves stopped fighting and stared at Simon and Letta.

"And if you're fighting over Letta, I need to put this matter to rest," Simon said. "She and I are mating, which means she's not going anywhere. There are no rules that state a fae bitten and changed by a wolf will become part of the pack that the attacking wolf belongs to. You don't have conclusive evidence that Hannah even belongs with either of your packs."

"And I don't want to belong to a pack where the only reason I'm wanted is because the leader wants her," Hannah said, pointing at Letta.

Letta only smiled at her. Simon was really hoping Hannah would find her pack and leave. Soon.

"I think she belongs with our pack," an older man said. "Hannah, I mean. We had a woman leave with a baby girl some years ago, and there was speculation that she had left a spouse who had been cheating on her, which is practically unheard of among wolves. She never returned. She didn't have any family with our pack. She had married into it. He never looked for her. We never found any evidence he was seeing another wolf. We think his mate just decided she'd made a mistake and didn't want to be with him. It's the only case I know of where one of our pack members left with a child, and Hannah is about the right age. That wasn't the baby's name, but I'm sure someone else would have changed it."

"And your claim to Letta?" Simon asked.

The leader smiled. "She has nothing to do with my claiming Hannah as one of our own. Just like we have no claim to the fae seers she changed. They're all welcome to join our pack as we can always use new blood as long as the wolves are hard workers like the rest of us, and agreeable."

Simon had no intention of telling him that Hannah was neither of those things. "It looks like you have a home finally, Hannah. I'm glad for it. If all the fighting is done here, we'll have dinner." Then he took Letta's arm and led her to the cottage.

CHAPTER 18

That night, they had a special celebration. It was usually the opening ceremony and whichever pack was hosting the event would provide the evening meal and entertainment. But tonight, Simon wanted to make it extra special.

"I'll be moving in with Valoran and Killington," Myla said, when they returned to the cottage. "Hannah will be leaving to join her pack, and the two of you will need your privacy."

Letta frowned. "We don't want you to leave the home that's been yours all along."

"I spoke with them and they're moving here to stay with you, Myla," Simon said. "Unlike me, they both like to cook. They can help you make meals. We'll move into their cottage."

"Are you sure?" Myla asked.

"Absolutely. This was the spot you chose for our cottage. You liked the way the summer breezes flowed through the windows."

Myla smiled. "You want their cottage with the river view."

"I didn't want to have to move you out when you've made this cottage your home. But I'm sure Letta will enjoy the view and sound of the river nearby."

"I will," Letta said.

"Our brothers don't care anything about being by the river, except they love to fish there as wolves. But it's not that far from your cottage anyway."

***

The feasting, drinking and dancing followed Simon's announcement that Letta was now his mate and co-pack leader. It made Letta feel as though she truly belonged to the pack after all the stuff that Gia and her brothers had pulled. They were eating and drinking, but seemed glum. The word must have spread about their traitorous deeds and they appeared to be outcasts among all the wolf packs. It served them right for what they had pulled and Letta realized this was a greater punishment then killing or banishing them.

Campfire stories were shared of the games won and lost of years past, young and old alike listening in or participating in the storytelling.

When Letta was growing up, her grandfather had told those he was raising all about the good deeds and the bad that their kin had done and she felt saddened to think that instead of playing competitive games with other scorpion fae clans, they had resorted to killing each off. She enjoyed hearing all the funny stories about the wolf packs.

Simon pulled her onto his lap and wrapped his arms around her, helping to warm her. He kissed her on the cheek, as if he realized she might feel somewhat like an outsider and he wanted to prove to her that she wasn't.

"The games are held to promote friendly and fun competition between the packs," he said to the gathered wolves. "May we always remember this as we start our one-hundredth wolf pack Gathering tomorrow."

Everyone cheered.

"Is it all friendly competition?" she asked Simon, surprised. She couldn't imagine some wouldn't feel grievances against the winning teams. They *were* fae.

"No. Sure, we have sore losers and tempers can flare, but for the most part, everyone has a good time. I just wanted to remind everybody what it is all about."

"Can we hear the lady's music?" one of the other pack leaders asked.

"Letta?" Simon asked her, and she appreciated that he just didn't expect her to play her music for the packs gathered there.

"Sure." She brought out her flute and began to play with all her heart, the heavenly melody filling the woods with mystery and a haunting beauty. She always felt swept away with her music as if she fell under its influence as much as everyone listening did.

When she finally finished the piece, everyone groaned to hear her end it. But the music was designed to end the night on a happy, relaxing note.

Tomorrow, if she played her music, she would play something that was riveting, making everyone want to move to the music. Not because her music forced anyone to do so. It was just that inspiring.

Simon helped Letta up and they retired to his brother's cottage that was now theirs. Ronan and Aegis had already moved Letta and Simon's clothes over, though Letta didn't have very many that she'd been able to bring with her.

"After the games, we need to go shopping for you," Simon said.

"Myla can go with me. You don't have to if you don't like to shop."

"No. I'd like to this time."

And she was glad he wanted to be with her for any reason.

***

That night at Ena and Brett's castle, the puppies howled in their little puppy voices. They were separated, Duchess with Muriel, and Duke with Jacob, and they were having a fit about it. Ena had put a pillow over her head, but she couldn't stand it. She finally got out of bed and paced. "Doesn't this bother you?"

Brett sighed. "They'll settle down."

"This is driving me crazy." She threw on her robe and left the chamber, stalked down to Jacob's room, and knocked on the door.

He answered it, the puppy cradled in his arms. "I'm so sorry, princess. I don't know what to do."

"Put the two of them together."

"Muriel won't let me have Duchess too."

Jacob following Ena, she took Duke and headed down to Muriel's chamber and knocked. Muriel quickly came to the door, Duchess at her feet. "Come on, Duchess. The two of you are going to sleep *or else*. They both will sleep with Brett and me. At least for a few days until they get used to their new pack and surroundings."

Jacob went back to his chamber for Duke's bed and he grabbed Duchess's bed out of Muriel's room, and she carried Duchess, then they all entered Ena and Brett's room with the beds and puppies.

Brett was sitting up in bed and watching them. "So *we're* taking the howling puppies *now*?"

"Yes, so we can get some sleep." She hoped.

The puppies curled up together in one bed and everyone watched them for a moment, before concluding that the puppies were staying put and not going to cry and whimper any longer.

"Night all," Ena said.

"Night, my lady," Muriel said.

"Night, princess," Jacob said, and he shut the door while Ena climbed back into bed.

"They better not make a peep." And they didn't. Not one little sound at all. Except for whimpers while having doggy dreams and a little bit of snoring, but that, Ena could ignore.

***

At the Wolf Mountain Gathering early the next morning, different kinds of food were served all over the square, including Maya's blueberry pancakes and maple syrup. Killington and Valoran helped her prepare stacks and stacks of them.

Wolves sampled them and other foods that had been made to feed everyone before the start of the games. Sausages, ham, sweet breads, and apples and oranges were served. Even hash browns, which Letta ate too many of.

Simon smiled at her. "I can see what you're going to vote on."

"The potatoes? Yes, and Myla's pancakes." Letta had gone back for seconds on those and honeyed ham slices too.

"The tug-of-war competition is first. We have several packs that have signed up for the game. The wolf pack that wins each of the competitions will face off with the winners later. The winner of those contests will begin to compete with each other after that, the freshest teams first until the final winning pack is announced. The music competition starts right before the nooning meal. You will play your music, won't you?" Simon asked.

"Yes. But just for fun. If I win, it would be nice, but I just like to play. I always played for our clan before we went to bed while the king told us stories. And also before the nooning meal to get everyone ready to tackle the rest of the day."

"Maybe you can do that with our pack."

"I would love to if everyone is agreeable. Well, except for Hannah. She's rarely agreeable so I wouldn't discount playing on account of her."

"She'll be leaving our pack soon."

"Oh, yes. I keep thinking she will be here forever. I hope she likes her new pack, but even if she doesn't, I'm glad she's going to be leaving."

Tomas approached them and Letta wondered what was up with him now. "Because of what we've done, my brothers and I weren't sure if we were allowed to participate in the tug-of-war games or not."

"Are you good enough at the game that you can help the pack win?" Letta asked before Simon had a chance to respond.

"Yes. We pull our weight." Tomas didn't seem perturbed with her for asking, though now that she was also a pack leader, he shouldn't be.

That was something she had to get used to also though. Helping Simon to make rulings, even though she was such a new wolf. "I'd say that you should participate then."

Simon agreed with her. "I don't see why not."

Looking serious, Tomas inclined his head, then hurried off in the direction of his brothers, both appearing eager to hear what had been decided concerning them.

"I think that's the first time I've seen him being

enthusiastic about anything since the collar incident," Letta said.

"I still don't trust them."

"Do you think they'll try to throw the game and lose?"

"No. They're too competitive for that, and the rest of the pack might just throw them out of the pack themselves. It was interesting to see that they were treated like omega wolves last night though, outcasts, the word having spread about their deceitfulness."

"I agree. If they thought to join another pack, they may be rethinking that plan."

"It's hurt their chances of securing a mating with a female wolf also," Simon said. "Not only for what they pulled, but because you removed their ability to fae transport."

"Serves them right."

"I agree."

"Are you going to help the pack win in the tug-of-war contest?" Letta asked.

"You bet. It's up now. I'll see you in a bit."

"Good luck." She found a place on top of a tall stack of rocks that were used to monitor games and other activities where she could stand and watch as the wolves lined up along the rope, getting ready to pull it until the rope went far enough that one side or the other would win. Each side had a mix of wolf builds, but most were hefty, muscled wolves—all male.

She noticed some distance across the square that two

more teams of wolves were competing in a tug-of-war contest.

One wolf howled, signaling the beginning of the contest.

The wolves began pulling, and she hoped no one lost any of their teeth over this. Though she'd seen dogs in tug-of-war contests with their pet owners or with each other, and they never did. She was surprised to see Gia climbing up to join her on top of the rock. Hopefully, she didn't plan to try and push Letta off, though if she did, Gia would be a dead wolf.

"I'm sorry about what we did to you and to Simon," Gia said.

Letta still didn't believe she was sincere. More that she was hoping if she said so, Letta might return her brothers' abilities to fae travel. Maybe, Gia thought if she and her brothers and Letta became friends, they would be out of the doghouse. But Gia had tried to kill her and her brothers had essentially tried the same thing with them, so Letta wasn't forgiving them anytime soon.

Letta didn't say anything, concentrating on watching her mate tug as hard as he could at the rope, to prove to the other packs that he and his pack had what it took to win.

"And I'm truly sorry about attacking you," Gia said.

Again, Letta didn't feel Gia was sincere about it. They wouldn't have hatched the scheme to try again, if she'd felt in the least bit sorry for what she'd done after she'd attacked Letta the first time.

"Are you really?" Letta asked, glancing in Gia's direction, not wanting to take her eyes off the competition, but the only way she could see Gia's expression and know for sure was to listen to her heart beating and smell her anxious scent, and to see the way her brown eyes were darkened, to truly tell what she felt. Letta didn't need a lie detector. Though the wolves and dragons could hear well, her scorpion fae could hear better than anyone. Which is why she could hear the faint beating of the two tiny babies that Ena was carrying or hear Gia's heart beating fast despite all the yelling— wolves encouraging wolves to beat the other packs for both competitions that were going on.

Gia didn't say anything, just waited to hear what Letta had to say about it, as if she knew she'd been found out and she had no way of proving otherwise.

"Suffice it to say, I have all kinds of abilities that no one knows about. Not even Simon or Myla. Just so you know."

Gia's jaw dropped, then she narrowed her eyes. She whipped around in a huff and headed down the rock as Letta saw Myla climbing up, looking worried. She cast Gia a dark look and passed her on the way up.

"Are you all right?" Myla asked. "I was worried when I saw her up here with you."

"She was just apologizing for what she and her brothers pulled."

"Do you believe her?"

"No. She just wants things to go back to the way

they were before she and her brothers ended up in the doghouse."

Myla frowned as she watched the competition down below. "Did you tell her you didn't believe her?"

"Yes. No sense in trying to play nice with her after what she and her brothers pulled. It's not fair to anyone else who has been welcoming to me and loyal to Simon."

"True. I still think my brother was too lenient with their punishment, though I hadn't expected our pack and others to ostracize them so. Even when Simon allowed them to participate in this game, many didn't agree."

"Except they want to win," Letta guessed.

"Right."

"Which proves a point. They can be useful to the pack. But we still don't completely trust them. Still, if I die, they lose their fae ability to transport forever and I think that will keep them from trying that again."

"They say that you were the one who told Ena she was having twins. Some have asked me how you knew that."

"I have exceptional hearing."

"So do we, and yet I couldn't hear her babies' heartbeats. Are you sure it isn't something else?" Myla asked.

"No. I heard their heartbeats."

"Well, then you have a new job, if you so choose to do it. I have to remember you're a pack leader now too and you are in charge."

Letta laughed. "You are always telling Simon what

to do."

"Yes, but he's my brother."

Letta smiled. "What is it that you'd like me to do?"

"A couple of our she-wolves hope they're pregnant. If you could tell, they would be extremely grateful."

Letta nodded. "Yes, I would be happy to do that job."

"And help with the deliveries? If it is true that they are both pregnant, they will deliver about the same time. Our healer won't be able to manage both."

"I'm a healer too. So yes, you know I'll help. I don't plan to be a figurehead of some kind. I want to help the pack in whatever way that I can. I need to prove that Simon made the right choice in picking me for a mate, when that meant I am also a pack leader because of it."

"Good. Everyone will be thrilled, our healer especially."

Then Myla got quiet as they watched the wolves still pulling on the rope. One on the other team stumbled, and then another tripped over him as Simon and his team were able to finally pull the rope in their direction. Wolves on the other team were beginning to trip over wolves as the others didn't move out of the way fast enough and the wolves that went down, lost their grip on the rope. It was a domino effect and soon after that, Simon and his team pulled the rope far enough onto their side to win the competition.

She and Myla cheered for their pack. She was glad they won, but she hoped they'd be good sports if they hadn't. When the other packs finished their competition, she played soothing music to placate the losing wolves and it was amazing how well it worked. She'd been taught how to do this by her aunt, a talent that, had it been used in centuries past, might have saved their people from annihilation. From then on, every generation was to learn the gift of music that would soothe the soul. Someday, she would pass it along to her own children.

Simon joined his sister and Letta up on the rock. "I can't believe how your kind could kill each other off, yet, you can use your music to smooth over things between losing teams."

"It's something that should have been used to stop the fighting, I agree, but for whatever reason, it wasn't."

Myla folded her arms as they watched the next packs compete in the tug-of-war competitions. "Gia was up here, trying to say she was sorry for what happened."

Simon raised his brow at Letta. She wrapped her arm around his waist. "She will never convince me of it."

"I didn't think so."

Then they saw a dark-haired man, about Simon's age, head for the rock they were standing on.

"Do you know him?" Letta asked.

"No. He's from one of the other packs. His pack won against the other in the tug-of-war competition."

"He looks intent on some business with you," Letta said.

"Do you want me to leave?" Myla asked.

Simon smiled at his sister. "No. You're fine

listening in on whatever the wolf has to say."

CHAPTER 19

When the man finally reached the top of the rock, he inclined his head with respect to Simon, Letta, and Myla. "I'm Barrow, and I understand Hannah was left in the human world, and just came into her abilities. I'm her brother." The dark-haired man smiled.

Simon didn't know the guy, except by sight at the games.

"You are not with the pack that claimed her already. Did you move to the new pack when you were older? The pack leader said nothing about her having a brother."

"I didn't know another pack had claimed her."

Okay, so that meant one of two things, Simon thought. This guy was lying, or the pack leader was. Gut instinct told him the pack leader had been sincere.

"Oh, I see the difficulty. She is my half-sister, though I would refer to her only as my sister. Our father was one and the same, our mothers different. Hannah's mother took her to the human world. My father, suffice it to say, had found a new mate when he was on a trip. He was wrong in doing so and Hannah's mother was ashamed and left her own pack."

"And your dad can verify that he is Hannah's father?"

"Of course. He's not at the Gathering, but I'll return and have him send word."

"Since Hannah's father abandoned her to be with your mother, Hannah belongs to her mother's pack." Though it would give Hannah a second option if she didn't care for her mother's pack and they didn't like her either. Still, Simon thought it sounded odd that the wolf was laying claim to her so all of a sudden.

"You know she was a fae seer before this?" Letta asked.

Barrow turned his gaze on her. "I do. She couldn't help what she was before she came into her powers. Not once she was abandoned by her mother."

"She had human foster parents," Letta said.

"Correct. She's not responsible for her actions when she lived there."

"It is good that you feel this way." Simon was studying Letta, trying to determine what she was seeing in Barrow. She had her head tilted to the side a bit, her eyes narrowed, as if she didn't believe the man. Likewise, Simon had reservations about him. But why claim Hannah for his own if she was nothing more than trouble.

"Have you had a lot of trouble with fae seers before? Have you lost pack members to them while visiting the human world?" Letta asked.

Barrow's expression darkened. "Of course. I'm sure we all have. It's a hazard of going to the human world and playing with fire."

"True," Simon said, but he suspected that Letta was getting at something else. Something darker.

"Why do you want to be her brother so bad? It seems to me that she'd feel some animosity for her father abandoning her and her own mother to want to have her live with your mother and you," Letta said.

"To make it up to her, naturally. To show that what happened between her mother and my father had nothing to do with the way I would feel about her. She's still my sister."

Letta smiled, but the look was pure cynicism, as though she knew Barrow was lying. "All right, then how would your father feel about this? You have come here seeking to take her into your pack and your father doesn't even know about it. Isn't that so? Did he ever look back? Ever wonder what had become of his daughter? Ever search for her? If she's happy with her mother's pack, I don't see why she would want to go to yours."

"Because she would have living family there. Me, Dad."

"And your mother?"

"She never had a daughter. She would welcome her."

Myla was studying Barrow as much as Letta was. Simon didn't think either Letta or his sister believed the wolf. "Unless Hannah says she wants to go home with you, she's going with her mother's pack leader. But we can discuss this with him and Hannah." He glanced at Letta to see how she felt about it.

"I agree. Her mother's pack has already stepped forward to take her in. And if we all talk and she decides she wants to go with you, we'll want proof first that your father is indeed her father and is willing to take her in."

"Why would I pretend some she-wolf I've never met is my own flesh-and-blood sister?" Barrow asked, sounding irritated.

That's what Simon wanted to know. He suspected Letta believed the wolf intended to use Hannah for some purpose. In line with Letta's questioning about fae seers, he thought she must think the wolf wanted Hannah to show him where her former fae seer friends were. And then what? Eliminate them? Maybe he thought she could show them how to get around to find more of the fae seers, but there was one problem with that. Even though they would have been her cohorts before, she was now one of the fae, showing off her fae aura, and they would know she wasn't one of them. Simon was certain Barrow had no intention of trying to find the fae seers to make friends with them.

"Have you spoken to Hannah yet?" Simon asked.

"No. Since you have been caring for her, and now knowing the other pack leader claimed her, I needed to come to you first."

"Good." At least Barrow had done that right.

Another couple of packs won rounds on the tug-of-war contest and cheers went up all around.

"We have one more round of four packs facing off on this contest. After that, if you're not participating in the next game, and Hannah's leader isn't, we'll meet with her and Silas," Simon said.

"Thank you." Barrow inclined his head and climbed down from the rock.

They waited until he was out of earshot and Simon asked Letta, "You suspect he wants to use Hannah to search out her co-conspirator fae seers and terminate them."

Letta nodded.

Myla frowned. "So he's not related to her? He just lied?"

"It could be. I'd like to learn if Barrow's father had another mate before Barrow can talk to him and convince him to say he's Hannah's father," Simon said.

"Who would you send?" Myla asked.

"Gia." Letta smiled. "She wants to prove she's loyal and above reproach, she can go. She can still transport herself and she can question the father."

"She'll have to be coached as to what to ask," Simon said.

Letta let out her breath. "I'll need to go. I'll be able to tell if he's lying or not. But I don't know my way around the packs. Would Gia even?"

"One of our brothers can go with you," Myla said. "I know Simon doesn't want to let you out of his sight for a second, but if you go, Killington can protect you. Maybe Valoran too. Simon has to stay for the Gathering as host pack leader."

"She's my pack leader mate. She needs to stay here too," Simon said.

"Well, if you really want to learn the truth, she needs to go," Myla said. "And before Barrow can send someone back to set up the ruse. Even while we're here arguing about it, he could be doing so."

"Don't your brothers need to be in the tug-of-war competition?" Letta asked.

Simon agreed with his mate. "Letta's right."

Myla folded her arms across her chest. "Someone else who isn't in the competition then."

"My strongest men are." Simon knew his sister worried about Letta, but she didn't have to go right now.

"Not your strongest then. Maybe Myla and her friend Crystal," Letta said.

Simon opened his mouth to object, but Letta kissed him, overriding his objection. "I have my magic too. Myla, do you want to go?"

"Yes. Crystal isn't flying in the winged wolf competitions until much later. We can see if she'll go with us. In the meantime, Simon can help us win the tug-of-war competition and set up a meeting with the pack leader, Silas, Barrow, and Hannah. We'll return as quickly as we can." Myla and Letta waited for Simon to agree.

He knew now that Myla wasn't going to step down from telling him how to run his pack, though he didn't mind. She often had great suggestions. He hugged Letta. "Go, but return as quickly as you can."

"We will."

Myla gave him a hug too and then she and Letta climbed down the rock. If it hadn't contained iron ore, they could have just transported themselves from there.

They quickly searched for Crystal and found her giving a pep talk to some of her friends.

"We need your help," Myla told Crystal, taking hold of her hand. "Now."

"You and Letta?" Crystal said.

"Yes, to uncover a mystery."

"I'm all for it. Let's go."

Letta really liked the winged wolf. She was full of adventure, no questions asked.

When the three of them transported and finally arrived at Barrow's wolf pack, they were met with wariness at first, but seeing they were three she-wolves with no male escort, some of the bachelor males appeared to be interested.

"We're looking for Barrow's father," Letta said. "I'm Simon's pack mate. This is his sister, Myla." Though she suspected they knew who she was since she knew how to find her way here. "And Crystal."

"Myla, Crystal," a man greeted them. "I've never heard of you before."

"She's new to the pack," Myla said. "Is Barrow's father around?"

"He just came back from a hunt. His cottage is on the other side of the village in that direction. What did you need to see him about? Nothing's the matter with Barrow, is it? Durbin would be beside himself to hear it."

"No, not at all. He's doing well in the tug-of-war competition. I imagine he'll be in competition against my mate later this afternoon," Letta said.

The man's face brightened. "Good to hear of it. I'll spread the word."

Letta smiled at him, and then she and the other ladies hurried off to find Barrow's father.

"What's this all about?" Crystal whispered.

"To learn if Durbin is truly Hannah's father, or Barrow lied about it," Letta whispered back.

Crystal frowned. "I can't imagine anyone wanting a wolf like that in their pack. I heard another pack claimed her."

Letta agreed wholeheartedly and she figured that once Hannah lived with anyone, they would learn the truth about her. Unless by some miracle she changed.

They saw a man out chopping wood and Letta was going to ask him if they could send them in the direction of Durbin's cottage, but when he saw them coming and straightened, he looked so much like Barrow, she figured he had to be his father.

"Are you Durbin?" Letta asked.

"Yeah," the man said, looking and sounding growly.

Letta smiled. "Hi! I understand that you had a daughter by a former wolf mate." She realized she should have waited until he set the axe down. Then again, it looked as though he had no intention of doing so because he had a job to finish.

"Where did you hear that?"

The problem was if she said his son, the dad might realize he needed to back him up. Otherwise, he might not want to admit he was a wolf who had abandoned his wolf mate.

"The daughter is with us, looking for her dad."

Durbin glanced at the other women with Letta.

"We didn't bring her with us to see you because we had to make sure if the rumor is correct or not. We didn't want to get her hopes up."

"I only have one mate, one son, and no daughter."

A woman came out of the cottage and said, "What's this all about?"

Did the woman know anything about Durbin's former mate? Or had Barrow lied about all of it for his own dark purpose. The only thing was that if he had lied and his dad wouldn't go along with the plan, especially if his mate strongly objected to it, Letta didn't know how he hoped to gain anything by it.

"Just chasing down an unfounded rumor. Thanks for your time." Then Letta and her friends fae transported back to the Wolf Mountain pack.

They were having relay races between wolf packs now, but Myla said, "I've got to help my brothers prepare the nooning meal. Are you going to tell Hannah about any of this?"

"I have to because I'm sure Barrow will speak to her before long. And I'm going to talk to the pack leader who claims she belongs to his pack also. Maybe Silas knows the truth."

"Okay, let me know."

"I will. And thanks, Crystal, for coming along."

"My pleasure. Any time you have a bit of sleuthing you need done, just let me know."

"Thanks." Letta headed to where she saw Simon watching the relay races to tell him what they'd learned.

He pulled her into his arms and kissed her. "I'm glad to see you back. What news?"

She explained what had happened. "Are you going to run in the relay races?"

"No. I'm saving my strength for the next tug-of-war contest between winners."

"Do you mind if I talk to the pack leader and Hannah about this situation?"

"No. I'd go with you, but I need to watch the games to show my support and make sure nothing gets out of hand."

"I'll let you know what I learn." Letta gave him a kiss, then headed off to find Hannah and the pack leader. She couldn't find Hannah right off, but she found Silas. He was giving his wolves a pep talk and glanced at her.

"Is there something wrong?" Silas asked.

"I just need to talk to you about something that came

up. Something concerning Hannah."

Silas joined her and they found a private place to talk. "What's this all about?"

"Do you know the wolf named Barrow?"

"Aye."

"Well, he claims Hannah is his sister."

"He does, does he?"

"Yes. He says his dad is Hannah's dad and he abandoned her mom, mated a new she-wolf, and had him. So Hannah is really his half-sister. I spoke with his father, but the man said it wasn't so. I didn't tell him his son was the one who claimed she was his sister. His mother came out of the cottage about that time. It could be that Durbin doesn't want to acknowledge that he had a former mate and daughter in front of his second mate and us, or he truly never had another mate, nor a daughter named Hannah."

"Why would Barrow make up this story then?"

"I don't know, unless, because she was a fae seer and knows more of them, he wants her to return there with him and he'll hunt them down."

"Have you discussed this with Hannah?"

"No. I came to you first." Mostly because Letta couldn't find Hannah. "I just want to do what's right for her." Letta couldn't believe she was trying to protect Hannah when she didn't even believe the woman would thank her for it. Then again, this is what her grandfather taught her, to show tolerance, and as a pack leader now, she really did have to try and keep the peace, like Simon was. "If she truly does have living family with another pack and they want her to stay with them, I just think she should have the option. But if Barrow does want her to stay with them, and she really is his sister, but the father doesn't want her to join his pack, nor does Barrow's mother, then we need to know that too."

"All right. Speak with Hannah. We'll leave it up to her."

"Thank you, Silas. We'll let you know what she decides when she decides it." Now, Letta just had to locate the willful fae.

CHAPTER 20

Simon was glad that Letta was trying to resolve this business with Hannah, showing she could take care of a situation as a pack leader, despite the misgivings she had about the woman. He was busy making sure that everything was running smoothly at the games. With this many wolves from different packs, there were bound to be some disagreements. Then he noticed Ronan hurrying to meet with him, his expression anxious.

"Is there something wrong?"

"I overheard Letta asking if anyone had seen Hannah. Is there something going on with the cantankerous woman?"

"Do you know Barrow?"

"Vaguely."

"He's said that Hannah is his sister."

"Oh, really."

"Letta located his father and questioned him about

it. She informed me his father says he was never mated before." Simon explained the rest. "So we're not sure what's going on. I need to be here for the games. Myla went with her earlier, but had to help prepare the next feast. Crystal went with them also, but she has winged wolf games she's participating in. When I asked if Letta needed any help with this, she said she would be all right as long as she was just among our pack members."

"After what happened to her because of Gia and her brothers?" Ronan scoffed. "Do you want me to go with Letta to help her with this if she is agreeable?"

It was important for Letta to feel as a pack leader she could sort out an issue regarding the pack for herself. But she was still a new wolf and new to the pack. If anything went sideways with this, Simon would always blame himself if he didn't have someone providing backup for her. He slapped his brother on the back. "Go, help her in any way that she thinks you can to speed up the process."

Ronan looked relieved and pleased all at once that Simon trusted him to assist and protect his mate. Simon watched his brother stalk off, but then he noticed that all his brothers were standing some distance away. Ronan headed straight for them, motioning with his hands to their territory, the brothers nodded, and then took off. Simon smiled. All his brothers had Letta's back. He couldn't have appreciated them more for it.

Then Simon saw Silas and wondered how the pack leader was feeling about Hannah possibly going to the other pack. He wondered about Silas's claim too. What if what *he* said wasn't true. That Hannah's mother had been part of his pack to begin with. Simon saw one of Silas's pack members, a woman who often won at the pie contests. She was at every Gathering because she won so often and she was old enough that she could have been Hannah's grandmother, so she'd know about a woman leaving with a baby earlier on. Simon walked off to join her and ask her about her pies and pack history.

"Emmaline, what kind of pies did you bring this time?" he said, drawing close to where she was setting up her pies.

"Chocolate cream pie is my latest creation." She beamed at Simon. "Did you want to be one of the first tasters?"

"You know I always have to vote for your pies. They're the best." Simon took a slice and ate it, loving the creamy, chocolaty taste. "I'll have to check out the others, but I think this is your best one ever." He always said that because they were always the best. "Are you sure I can't talk you into joining our pack?" He asked her the same question every year, knowing she wouldn't leave her own pack behind, but he loved to tease her and she smiled with pleasure.

"You only say that because you want me to win the pie competition for *your* pack."

"My wolves would be at your shop every day, eating your meals and keeping you well paid."

She smiled again. "Thank you for your kind words, Simon. You are a charmer. Other packs hate that I usually win, beating out the competition. But you are always so gallant and understanding. Even when your own sister is competing against me."

"See, that is part of my ploy. You can teach her how to make pies like you do."

Emmaline laughed. "Then I would be competing against myself."

Simon smiled, then he changed the subject to the one he needed to discuss. "Silas said you had a woman who left the pack with a baby girl some years ago. Her mate had abandoned her."

Emmaline frowned. "I know Silas has been saying so, but I don't recall anything of the sort. Now, I did hear rumors about Rupert's pack having a situation like that."

"And the woman's mate? Where did he end up, do you know?"

She shrugged. "I wouldn't know that, but I'd check with Rupert's pack about the mother and baby. Maybe they'll even know about the father of the baby."

"Thanks, I will." Simon wanted to ask why Silas would make up the story if Hannah's mother hadn't been with the pack, but he didn't want to antagonize Silas should he get word Simon had questioned Emmaline about that. Simon went in search of Letta or his brothers to tell them to ask any of the older members of Rupert's pack if they knew about Hannah and her mother.

He wasn't having any luck finding Letta, but he saw Myla setting out the dishes for the nooning meal. She smiled brightly at him. "I saw you talking to Emmaline.

I know you're going to vote for her pies over mine."

He laughed. "But your veal always has my vote. I tried to talk her into teaching her secret recipe and tips for making her pies, but you know she won't budge."

"I think she will take her knowledge to the grave. I've asked if she has anyone that she's apprenticing in her pack, but she's not. She says it's because she doesn't go by a recipe. She adds a pinch of this, a little of that. I know what she means."

"That's a shame. Have you seen Letta or any of our brothers?"

"Not for a while. What's up?"

"I learned some news about Silas's pack. Hannah might not belong to them after all. Emmaline says that she thinks Rupert's pack might actually be where Hannah and her mother originated."

"No. What is going on? I thought Rupert's pack said she wasn't one of theirs."

"Yeah, they did. Maybe her attitude gave them heartburn and they didn't want her in the pack."

"So why do Barrow and Silas want her?"

"Your guess is as good as mine. If you see any of our brothers or Letta, let them know what's happened, all right?"

"Okay, yeah, sure. What are you going to do?"

"See if I can locate any more of Silas's older wolves and Rupert's also to learn if anyone for sure knows that the wolf was with their packs."

"Good luck, Simon. I hope it doesn't mean we're

stuck with her."

"Well, we still have two people who want her."

Myla smiled at him. "I know you won't give her up unless you know for certain she's going to be treated right, despite what she did to me and the others."

Simon inclined his head to his sister and searched the area for any sign of his brothers or Letta, or the people he could question to sort this all out.

***

Back at Brett and Ena's castle, Ena was thrilled to get some news about the prized goat she'd given to Queen Viviana and to share it with her mate. "The queen's new goat won the competition. You see? Finding the goat but not getting paid for its return has its own rewards. She was delighted and gloated about it in front of the former owner, who was out-of-sorts that he lost the contest with his new 'prized' goat that couldn't beat the other."

Brett gathered Ena in his arms and kissed her. "And I hear she is much pleased with the gift of koi you made her."

"Hmpf. She was supposed to pay for those."

"Well, I have good news. We are officially the queen's choice for taking on quests. If anyone in her employ needs a dragon's help, they must come to us first. So I agree. A little bit of generosity pays back in a big way."

Ena sighed. "All right. Then I"—she frowned as Duke began to squat—"He's going to potty on the floor."

Brett turned into his dragon and lifted the startled puppy off the floor, as Ryker hurried to open the door for Brett.

"Just in the nick of time," Ryker said, amused. "I've cleaned up one too many messes of late."

"Hurry, Ryker, grab Duchess—oh, forget it." Ena shifted into her dragon and took hold of the puppy and joined Brett outside. She set the puppy on the grass and shifted. "We're going to have to schedule puppy sitters throughout the day until they're housebroken, and they're leashed-trained."

They'd been shifting in front of the puppies to let them know their other appearance so they wouldn't be scared by it, even though the puppies could still smell that they were the same person.

"That sounds like a good idea to me. I was thinking we should take a vacation before the babies come. Once they're here, we'll feel more tied down," Brett said.

"Human world? Or our world? Maybe take on a quest to pay for the trip?" As if they didn't have enough treasure to pay for vacations a hundred times over. And if they took the vacation in the human world, they wouldn't have to pay for anything.

They saw Halloran in his green dragon form headed their way and Ena wondered what he wanted now. Halloran dropped into the courtyard, shifted, and smiled. "Taking the pooches for a walk, I see. Somehow, I never imagined Ena taking in puppies. Then again, my sister's always taking in strays."

"Don't you have a job to do for your queen, Dragon at Arms?" Ena asked, annoyed.

"I do. The queen has an important mission for you."

"We were—" Brett started to say.

"Good. We'll do it." Ena was always ready for a mission. "What is it this time?" She was thinking maybe the treasure they'd receive from the task would help pay for their trip and they wouldn't have to borrow from their treasure pile.

"She wants housebroken puppies. She heard all about yours." Halloran cast her an evil smile.

Ena couldn't believe it!

"It's the highest form of compliment, you know. That she wants to copy everything you do."

"But housebroken."

"Two. Yes. What were you going to say, Brett?" Halloran asked.

"We were going on a vacation before Ena has the babies."

"No problem. You will have months before that happens."

"I want to ask Max and Bryan if they'd like to help me with this," Ena said. "But they're at the Gathering."

"They can help you later. These two can be the queen's since they have a head start on housebreaking."

"No way," Ena said. "Duke and Duchess are part of our family now."

Halloran smiled. "I think Ena's maternal instincts are coming to bear. Good show and good luck." Halloran shifted into his dragon. The puppies woofed at him, acting as though they were protecting Ena and Brett, and then Halloran flew off.

"I can go with you to the pet shop this time," Brett said.

"What if you wanted to bring home more puppies?"

"I think we have our hands full with these—well, and the queen's, now, once we pick them up."

Looking panicked, Jacob came running outside, then saw them with the puppies. "Oh, I was afraid we'd lost Duke and Duchess."

Ena smiled. "No, but we're going to need a puppy-watching schedule. And the queen wants us to housebreak two puppies for her."

Jacob's eyes grew big. "To pick them out for her too?"

"Yes. We'll wait until Mark and Bryan are done with the Gathering, but I'm going over there and give them a heads-up."

"I'll go with you," Brett said. "I'd like to see how they're doing at the games. Of course they might not be allowed to participate, as new as they are to all of this."

"I'll take care of Duchess and Duke then and have a puppy schedule drawn up," Jacob said and picked up each puppy and headed inside.

"Shall we?" Ena took Brett's hand and they transported to the Wolf Mountain pack territory. When they arrived, she was caught up in the excitement just like all the contestants and observers were. The dragon games were just like that for them.

She couldn't see Mark and Bryan for all the people here and she said to Brett, "Let's shift and soar over the area to see if we can locate them."

He agreed and they shifted, then took flight.

She saw wolves in tug-of-war competitions and other wolves hurriedly searching for hidden objects. She thought that was fun and wondered if they couldn't add something like that to the dragon games, but it would have to be objects hidden high above the ground for the dragons to find. Then she saw a man arguing with Hannah, and at first, Ena thought the woman had caused some trouble. Ena didn't know the man, or whether or not he was in Simon's pack or another.

But when he grabbed Hannah's arm and she tried to pull away, Ena went into dragon-protector mode. It was so overcast, Ena and Brett's dragon forms didn't cast a shadow. Neither Hannah nor the man saw Ena coming. In her peripheral vision, she saw Brett headed in the same direction.

Before the man could transport Hannah somewhere else, if he intended to, Ena swooped down and grabbed Hannah by the shoulders and carried her off. She screamed in terror, but realizing it was Ena, she shut up. Ena hovered above the top of a large rock and released Hannah. Brett brought the man with him and set him down as Ena settled on the rock and shifted.

"Okay, what's this all about?" Ena asked.

Brett landed on the rock, but remained in his dragon

form, a deterrent for the man if he thought to grab Hannah again.

They knew Hannah could be totally at fault, so they knew to expect anything.

"Barrow lies about being my brother! His father denies I'm his daughter! And another pack leader claims I'm one of his people when his people say I'm not. And another pack won't claim me, when pack members say I'm part of the pack."

Ena smiled. She couldn't help herself. If Hannah had been likeable, Simon would most likely have convinced her to stay with his pack.

"There!" Letta said from down below, pointing at them sitting high up on the rock. She was with Simon and his brothers and they appeared to be concerned for Hannah.

They all had to climb up on top of the rock and Ena was eager to hear what was going on.

"This man had accosted Hannah," Ena said first.

"Apparently," Simon said, "a couple of packs have some grievances with fae seers, and they have the notion that they can use Hannah to go after them."

"But she's not truly a member of their packs," Letta said. "Thank you for coming to Hannah's aid."

"It looks like we have confirmed that she belongs to another pack," Simon said.

"That doesn't want me," Hannah said.

"Why?" Ena asked. Unless they knew her personally, she didn't understand why a pack wouldn't want to take in a former member who had been abandoned in the human world for who knew what reason really. And Hannah had nothing to do with that.

Hannah brushed away tears. "I don't belong anywhere. Even *you* don't want me back."

"Is that no wonder?" Ena wasn't about to sugarcoat Hannah's circumstances. She wasn't going to roll over and say Hannah could return to her employ, when she wouldn't work at all.

"You can stay here with our pack until we sort it out," Simon said. "But Ena's right. You have to earn your keep, just like everyone else does."

Bryan and Mark joined them then, Bryan saying, "We overheard some of the conversation. Man, we can't believe how much we can hear with our wolf senses. Anyway, Mark and I have been offered jobs to create gardens for various people—like the dragon shifter, Alton and his mate. So if you want to help us plant and pull weeds and remove existing plants to make way for new plants, you can come to work for us. But you won't be able to get away with what you used to pull. Not now that you're a fae like everyone else here. It was one thing when you were a mopey human fae seer. You're not that any longer. Not that it gave you a good excuse to shirk your responsibilities before."

"Yeah, we're willing to give you a chance to help us create beautiful gardens, but it means lots of hard work. If you don't want to help, you'll have to find work somewhere else," Mark agreed.

Ena suspected Bryan still felt some responsibility for Hannah since he was the one who wanted to take her to the fae world with them. She was glad he offered. She hoped Hannah would finally get her act together.

"By the way, when you're free, would you like to go with me and return to the human world to pick up some more puppies?" Ena asked Mark and Bryan.

"You want more underfoot?" Mark asked, sounding surprised.

"No, Queen Viviana wants them."

Bryan and Mark laughed. "Don't get anything else new or she'll want it too," Mark said.

"I want to go too," Hannah said.

Not once since they'd taken Hannah with them to the fae world had she been allowed to return to the human world. But now that she had fae traveling abilities, she could go there whenever she liked. They couldn't stop her, unless they made her wear a fae collar, but why bother?

Ena just wasn't sure that it was safe for them to take her with them.

Mark and Bryan were watching Ena, trying to decipher which way she would go on it. She finally nodded. "All right, but you listen to whatever any of us have to say."

"I will. I know how dangerous it can be if fae seers see us. Even if my friends, former friends, were in the area, I would be on their target list now," Hannah said.

"We're free now if you want to go," Mark said.

"After the trials. The queen will have to wait to take her puppies home after they're housebroken anyway. We'll take care of that part, but I just thought you'd like to go with us to pick out the puppies and select whatever else they need before we turn them over to the queen."

"Yes," both Mark and Bryan said.

Even though Hannah didn't chime in, she looked just as eager to go with them.

"Do you mind if I go with you this time?" Brett asked.

"We'd love to have you come along. You can help run interference if anyone thinks we haven't 'paid' for the merchandise."

"I could help," Letta said.

"If you go, I'll go too. You're not thinking of picking up a puppy of your own, are you?" Simon asked.

Letta just cast him a devious smile and Ena suspected that's just what she had intended.

"We could just get a puppy somewhere around here, you know," Simon told her.

"I know, but where's the fun and excitement in that?" Letta said.

"All right, it's settled. Return to my castle when you have finished your games and we'll go on a puppy hunt," Ena said.

Then she and Brett shifted, flew off the rock as dragons, and headed home.

***

"Do you want a puppy?" Simon asked Letta. He

knew that a dog would soon become one of the pack, even though no one in his pack had one. A few fae had them for pets, cats, and birds too, but most had them if they were working animals. Cherished still, but useful in some way, other than just a companion.

"Sure? Why not? They make cherished companions."

"You have *me*."

Letta laughed. "Of course I do. I grew up around dogs. When I had to live with my grandfather, he wouldn't allow me to take my dog with me. My brother took care of her until she died."

Simon nodded. "A puppy it is."

"Maybe two so that she's not lonely."

He smiled. As soon as Ena had mentioned getting puppies for the queen, he saw the interest in Letta's expression. He would get her anything to make her happy. "You'll have to be in charge of puppy training. I'll help, but I haven't the foggiest idea how to take care of a puppy. I mean, as wolves, we're similar but we're also fae."

Letta laughed. "Good thing too."

Simon was called up for the final tug-of-war contest between wolves and he hoped they won, but he'd already won the greatest contest of all—Letta's heart and his pack leader mate.

CHAPTER 21

More music was playing in the background, but when Simon was in the final tug-of-war contest to determine which pack won for the celebration, Letta stood on top of the rock and played her music, encouraging both wolf teams to pull their hardest. She could have inspired just her pack, but she didn't want to influence the outcome. She just wanted everyone to enjoy the rivalry between the last two winning teams before the true winner was decided.

Then she saw the man who said he was Hannah's brother talking to Hannah. Letta hoped he wasn't trying to bribe or convince Hannah to return with him to the human world so that he could eliminate the fae seers she knew. Letta didn't know what came over her, but she wanted to help Hannah find her family or learn what had happened to them.

And she was even thinking Hannah should stay with

them and if they could, they would teach her to be one of them—which was ironic, since Letta hadn't started out as one of them either. But at least she'd been a fae all along.

Then Letta noticed Myla and Crystal were standing near Hannah as if they were there to protect her since Myla's brothers were all in the tug-of-war contest. Then Gia came up to join Letta on the rock.

Letta didn't stop playing her music but nodded a greeting.

"You probably wonder what Barrow wants with Hannah. He insists he's her brother, that his father lied about her because being a wolf and cheating on his mate was such a terrible thing to do." Gia frowned at the wolves in the contest. "Are you helping both sides? I thought you were playing to help just our side."

Since Gia had tried to take Letta down so she still had a chance to mate Simon, Letta figured the woman wouldn't get it. Letta played the music to encourage all the players. The competition would remain with the players, and the best, or luckiest, would win.

Letta's heart stuttered when she saw Roland slip and fall, losing hold of the rope. That was a disaster in the making. As soon as he did, she knew a bunch of the wolves could trip over him or lose their grip, like a domino effect that she'd seen earlier with competing teams. But Roland jumped back into the fray before they lost any ground and as if to save face, he tugged so hard, growling so loud, that two of the wolves on the other team lost hold of the rope.

The feeling that the rope was now navigating in the direction of Simon's team must have given them encouragement and they tugged all the harder, putting their teeth and backs into it, their paws digging into the ground to keep their footing.

Though she hoped their pack won, naturally, she would be just as glad if their pack lost and were still of good cheer to show how it was done. Two more wolves on the other team fell and one of the wolves on Simon's team lost his grip on the rope. She could see wolves losing their grips and trying to get another good bite hold on the rope, which was how they would lose the battle, if too many were doing it at the same time. They really had to do this as teamwork. Perfect for wolf packs in competition.

The opposing team would tug even harder when they could see or feel the other team's members letting up on the rope.

All the wolves were getting tired, but Simon's team was trying to take advantage of the advances they'd made and tugged all the harder, inching the rope in their direction. It could still go either way. One or two wolves could fall and catastrophe could strike and the team would lose.

Two wolves on Simon's team let go at the same time and the opposing team gained the ground they'd lost, but then the wolves grabbed hold of the rope with a better grip and Simon's pack pulled harder. She didn't think anyone was going to last as tired as they looked, but then the rope inched little bit by little bit back in Simon's direction. If they could just keep it up, they wouldn't have to win by a big pull, just little, steady, sure pulls. And that's what they did. No matter how much the other team tried to regain the ground, they just didn't have the energy, and when Simon's team made it to the point where the other team crossed the line, her pack won!

She continued to play her music in celebration and in a way to smooth over hard feelings among the losing team members and with Simon's team until everyone was cheering and congratulating each other.

Simon had shifted and climbed up the rocks to reach her, eyeing Gia warily, who was still standing next to her.

"I was just telling your co-leader about what Barrow is up to with regard to Hannah." Then Gia headed down the rocks.

Simon wrapped his arms around Letta's shoulders and called out to the assembled packs. "Let the feasting begin."

Letta realized then that the aroma of bread baking, shellfish and wild boar cooking was filling the air.

Simon leaned down to kiss Letta's lips and she wrapped her arms around his neck. "Thanks for the beautiful music. It helped us to win."

She smiled. "It was to help both teams to concentrate and win."

He still seemed worried about what Gia was up to though. "Was that all that Gia wanted?"

"She wanted to know why I didn't play music that would help you to win."

"You did. It helped me, anyway."

"Having me watch you would have the same effect. I know you well enough to realize you had to prove to me you could win the challenge. Not just for the pack. But for me."

Simon chuckled. "How would it look to my new mate if I couldn't lead my pack and win the battle? Everyone else knows I can do it, but this is the first time you get to see it for yourself. Though if we had lost, I would have been a good sport about it. In the end, that's what everyone remembers about the games."

***

There were three more days of competitions and Myla and Letta enjoyed seeing the winged fae in competitions, similar to what the dragon shifter competitions were like—retrieving objects from trees and returning the fastest, only they did it in relay teams. Again, packs did things together so even in games they showed they could work as one.

Crystal's team came in first and Letta was glad for her. Letta had heard grumblings about giving her first place on her magical music, but she really didn't compete and didn't want to accept any accolades. She just loved sharing her music for the pure enjoyment of it.

At the end of the festivities, the pack leaders of the various packs that had participated paid her tribute for making the games so much more festive and thanked her for her generosity.

The next morning after the final feast the night before, the visiting wolves packed up their belongings and the competitions would take place in Barrow's pack territory next year.

Barrow spoke one last time to Hannah in private and then he left with the others of his pack.

Likewise, Silas seemed to be making a last-ditch effort to convince Hannah to leave with him and join his pack, but she shook her head. Then when he left, Hannah saw Letta and Simon watching her and she joined them.

"It's awful to only be popular because those who want to be my friends want to use me," Hannah said.

"You're welcome to stay with us as long as you do your fair share of the work and are pleasant enough," Letta said, having discussed the matter with Simon, Myla, and their brothers and sisters earlier. They had agreed to give her another chance.

"At least you don't want me to stay here because you need me to help you kill fae seers."

"You must feel that they could be just like you," Letta said. "And more than that, I'm sure you still feel some sense of friendship with them, feeling you were doing the right thing at the time. Getting rid of the aliens who were out to get you because of your ability to see them—us."

"Yeah. I mean, I was human for so long, Mark and Bryan and Brett too. I really couldn't see myself being a fae seer one minute and then a fae the next, let alone that

I could be a wolf shifter. It didn't matter to me that Brett and Alicia had changed. Mark, Bryan, and I hadn't, so I just figured we weren't the same as the others. Even now, I wonder if they might never have been fae if I hadn't turned Bryan. I have to admit I don't regret it though."

Letta raised her brows.

Hannah shrugged. "They're happy being fae. You're fae and have always been fae. I heard you telling some others that you'd lived among the humans for some years and had been lucky not to come across too many fae seers. But you had your abilities."

"Not right away. But I know what you mean. I knew what I was, a fae, right from the beginning. I never thought I was a fae seer. When we're younger, we don't have an aura so that if we end up in the human world, we're protected."

"Right. So living among the humans who couldn't see the fae made us stand out. But because we could see the fae, we had to be so careful not to let on that we could. If you didn't have an aura when you were little, how did you manage to prove to the fae visiting the human world that you were one of them?"

"I was young enough. Once you're in your teens though, it was time to move back to the fae world or deal with fae seers. Which I did."

"Okay, then we came here, Bryan and Mark and I, and we were in the minority. Brett too, until he came into his abilities. Not only that but the fae knew we were fae seers who had killed fae."

"But Ena and her staff didn't treat you poorly for it." Even though Hannah hadn't been an agreeable member of the staff either.

"I...I just felt I didn't fit in. Even as a fae, I'm still different because I'm a new wolf to a pack. I was in and out of foster homes. I was angry that my parents had abandoned me. And I didn't get along with anyone. Not until I met other fae seers like myself. I respect you because you weren't a wolf either, even though you've been a fae all along. But your scorpion heritage evoked negative feelings among other fae too, like my being a fae seer."

"But you *are* a fae, and have always been a fae, not a fae seer. So you just need to embrace that you are and move forward."

"I'm trying. Bryan and Mark had lots of adventures with the dragon fae before I arrived. Helping them to fight their battles even. Even though they were fae seers like me, they just seemed to fit in—maybe because of all the role-playing they did at Dungeons and Dragons' games. They were already good at sword play and dressing in character. I never did that. Not even to go trick-or-treating at Halloween. My foster parents didn't believe in any of that."

Letta smiled. "Then we'll have to go this year."

"You do that here?"

"Where do you think that all came from? *Trick* or treat? One of our favorite holidays. Same with April Fool's Day."

Hannah offered her first genuine smile that Letta had seen since she'd met her. Letta glanced at Simon. He smiled back. "I haven't done that in years."

"I always return to see my brother and we go together. I use a little magic, of course. Glamor magic too. No one knows what age we are then."

"Sounds good to me," Simon said. "We could even be a whole gang of kids hitting all the homes."

"I can't wait. Two weeks." Letta loved Simon for wanting to go along with it. And she thought Hannah might just feel like she belonged after all.

"I...I want to stay here with your pack. Even though I did wrong in biting everyone, I was just lashing out. I was just out of my head. Terrified of what I'd become. Not like Gia did to you. Every chance I get, I try to overhear anything she and her brothers are saying, just in case they plan another attempt to kill either of you."

"I doubt they will now, unless they don't care if they get their fae travel abilities back or not."

"Oh. True. I know Ena told you I wouldn't work in the gardens. I hate gardening. I'm just not cut out for it. I grow weeds really well and everything we are supposed to grow dies under my touch. But I'm good with animals if you want me to help with your puppies."

"We raise sheep and alpacas for their wool. Maybe you can help sheer the animals, clean the fur, and help sell it to the weavers. I heard one of the women who works with the sheep mated a wolf and moved off to his pack."

"Uhm, okay. I had two dogs and a cat when I was growing up. Well, they weren't mine, but I helped take care of them."

"All right, then. So why don't you try that out." Letta had never considered the possibility that Hannah just hadn't liked the work she'd been assigned to do, but that given the chance to do something she liked, she might be more hardworking. Or not. Time would tell.

Simon said, "If you're ready to go with the others to the pet store, it's time."

"And we need to pick out costumes too," Letta said, eager to do Halloween this year. She wondered just how many of the pack members would end up going with them. But she thought Gia's brothers shouldn't be able to participate. No sense in having to carry them around to the human world after what they pulled.

***

When they met up with Ena and Brett, Ena didn't seem particularly pleased to see Hannah, but Simon was glad that Letta had been willing to talk to the willful woman and maybe learn why she was the way she was.

"We're going to pick out costumes too and go trick-or-treating," Letta said, sounding so eager, Simon knew that's why he loved her.

Trick-or-treating, playing fae games, it just wasn't something he or his kind usually did. But he would throw it open to anyone in the pack who wanted to go with them.

"Oh, my, now that sounds like fun." Ena glanced at

Brett to see his take on it.

As far as Simon knew, Ena was a real workaholic, and playing, unless it earned her treasure, wasn't something she usually did.

"It's up to you, honey," Brett said. "We can put off our vacation until after Halloween. But won't we be a little old?"

"Glamor will do the trick," Ena said.

"And we might even find a Halloween party to go to that we can crash where we won't have to hide our ages," Letta said.

"Who all is going?" Ena asked.

"Everyone from the pack who wants to," Simon said. "Except for Gia's brothers. They're not returning to the human world until they have their fae transporting abilities back." There wasn't any reason to give them a free ride.

"Okay. Are we going together?" Ena asked, looking pleased. Then she smiled. "You probably didn't expect me to say I'd go. I've never done it before, but I have the Gothic girl look down pat, and I'm ready. Instead of gold and baubles, we'll just get lots of treats."

"We can go as dragon slayers...uhm"—Mark's cheeks reddened—"forget I said that. We can go as dragon tamers—"

Bryan laughed. "We used to play Dragons and Dungeons' games. Mark, stop talking while you're behind."

"I will go as a mighty wizard," Brett said.

"You're supposed to dress up as something you aren't normally," Letta said, laughing. "I'll be a fairy princess."

Simon smiled at her. "You *are* a fairy princess."

"No," Mark said. "Get outta here."

"Her grandfather is the king of the scorpion fae."

"Well, there's more to you than meets the eye," Ena said.

"But wolves don't have titles, so I don't need it."

"I would sure love to be a princess," Hannah said.

Ena rolled her eyes, and Simon suspected the way she'd acted at her castle and not doing any work made it appear Hannah thought she was already a princess.

"Everyone ready to go? Puppies here we come," Ena said.

CHAPTER 22

At the pet store, Brett told Ena they needed to get the same breed of dogs that they already had brought home, or the queen could throw a fit.

Simon was letting Letta pick out the breed of dog she wanted. She was looking at puppies that were of a larger breed. Great Danes and Irish wolfhounds. "Wolfhounds," she said. "They were used to take down wolves in the human world, but ours will be part of the pack."

"Wolfhounds it is." He was thinking of two males, but when she got a male and female, he suspected what she was up to. Especially once she learned they were not from the same litter.

"We can raise them and sell off their puppies to others who would like to have one."

"Unless you can't part with them," Simon said.

Letta smiled up at him. "Well, then we can only sell

them to pack members so they're close by."

Mark and Bryan shook their heads. "That means bigger bedding, bigger chew toys, bigger everything," Bryan said.

Hannah was playing with the puppies in a pen.

"Something seems to have changed with her," Ena said privately to Simon.

"I believe we've come to an understanding. And she's going to stay with the pack." Simon folded his arms, watching the woman. Then he stared at her aura. "What...the..."

"Her...her aura changed," Ena said.

Brett glanced at Letta who was picking out the color of bedding she wanted for the puppies. Her aura. Silvery green. The same as Hannah's now.

"What just happened?" Brett asked.

"It appears Hannah's parents were two different fae kind. A wolf and a—" Simon said.

"Scorpion fae," Ena said. "You're really going to have your hands full with that, if she's a magic user like Letta is."

Simon sighed. Now they were really stuck with Hannah no matter what. Maybe that's why she was so warlike—one of the scorpion fae, only she had just now come into her actual abilities. Letta would have to train her how to deal with them, if she was a magic user like her.

Letta had one of the puppies in her arms as she joined him and Ena and Brett and saw their worried expressions. "What?"

"Your aura and Hannah's are the same now. She had the same wolf aura as the rest of the wolves before this," Simon said.

Letta turned around to look at Hannah. "Oh. My. God." Letta's mouth gaped. The puppy licked her cheek.

"Yeah, will she have any magical abilities?" Simon asked. It could be a blessing or more trouble than they could handle.

"Yeah, and how. Okay, then she's not sheering sheep. She'll have to be my apprentice until she can control her magic skills."

"I think it might be time to leave, just in case," Ena warned.

"Uh, yeah, I agree." Letta cuddled her puppy. "Mark and Bryan's hands are full. You need to get your puppy, Simon."

He'd never raised a pet before. He smiled and took the other one she had picked out.

And then they were off with their furry bundles of joy and all the stuff they needed to take with them as if the puppies were royalty themselves.

Once Simon and the rest of his wolves had returned to the pack territory, the dragons having gone home with Jacob and the queen's pups, Letta had to speak with Hannah.

"Come on," Simon said, ushering them into the cottage.

Mark and Bryan came also, loaded down with puppy

beds and all the rest.

"The two of you have puppy detail," Simon said to Mark and Bryan. "Why don't you take them outside and show them where to potty."

"Yeah, sure thing," Mark said, taking the female from Letta and Bryan took the male from Simon and headed outside.

Hannah had set up the puppy's bed near a fireplace, and their dishes near the kitchen and filled their water bowl.

"Hannah, we need to talk," Letta said gently.

"My aura looks like yours now." Hannah appeared not to know what to think of it.

"I'm sorry that your abilities are changing again. And it'll mean you'll have to learn to control them."

"I'm...I'm one of you, the scorpion fae?"

"It appears that way."

Hannah's eyes widened. "The magic? Will I have magic?"

"Yes. But like me, you'll have to practice using spells for them to really be powerful or useful."

Simon grabbed Hannah's arm, her face had turned so pale and he was afraid she was going to collapse. He led her to the living area and helped her to sit.

"I'll help you to control your spells, but you can only use them for doing good."

"Unless someone's trying to kill me, like what happened with Gia," Hannah said, but she sounded like she was asking, not really telling Letta what she would do if she was faced with such a situation.

"For defensive purposes. Yes."

"Will Mark and Bryan turn into a scorpion fae?" Hannah asked, rubbing her forehead in bewilderment.

"Only if one of their true parents was one, which must be the case with you. And it may mean that you might even be related to me."

Hannah brightened. "A princess?"

Letta rolled her eyes this time.

Simon smiled at Letta's reaction. But what if Hannah was related to Letta and a princess? He could see living with her could be insufferable. Or, if she belonged with the scorpion fae, maybe the king could tutor her for a while, and knock some sense into her. Though Letta had said that once she came of age, she had to leave. But maybe, due to the circumstances, the king would take Hannah in until she had her magic under control.

"Should we take her to see your grandfather?" Simon asked Letta.

"Yeah. That was my very thought. You seem to have your wolf under control, Hannah," Letta said. "We need to get your magic under control, and we can learn what my grandfather might know about you and your family."

Wringing her hands, Hannah seemed anxious.

Letta smiled. "He appears to be a young boy, but he's ancient. I'm sure he'll like you."

"You're…you're going to leave me there?"

"You couldn't have a better and more patient teacher than the king."

"But...I won't be coming back here?" Hannah had tears in her eyes and looked overwhelmed with grief, like this was the story of her life as she was pawned off on yet another "foster" family.

"You'll be returning to us. If you ever want to find a mate. When we come of age, we leave our kind behind. But you have a home with us. Always. You just have to work hard to prove you have the magic under control. You can live with us when you have some control and I'll work on it with you. You can return to see him later to learn more advanced skills."

"What...what about Halloween?"

"You...might not be ready by then to safely visit the human world."

Hannah looked crestfallen.

Letta took her hand and pulled her up from the couch, then gave her a hug. "We can do it again next year and every year thereafter until you're tired of doing it. We can play April Fool's jokes on humans before then. You just have to learn your skills, so you don't hurt anyone, fae, humans, the puppies even. It takes years of practice to get as good as me, but you'll be able to have some control once my grandfather and I teach you how to control your spells."

Mark and Bryan were laughing outside, then both came in with the puppies. "No leashes for them. That's something we'll have to get them used to."

"We have a mission," Simon said. "So the puppies are in your care until we return."

"Hannah's too?" Bryan asked.

"She's going with us."

Both Mark and Bryan frowned at them, as if suspecting they were getting rid of Hannah.

"You might have noticed her fae aura is now the same as Letta's," Simon said.

They both looked at one another and then at the ladies. Their eyes rounded. "Hannah's a magic user?" Bryan asked.

"Half scorpion fae, and yes," Simon said. "We're taking her to see Letta's grandfather to learn if he'll teach her some skills to control her magic."

"Oh, wow," Mark said. "Okay. We'll take care of the puppies."

"We'll name them when we return," Simon said. "We need to do this at once, before anything untoward happens."

***

Letta hoped her grandfather would take Hannah in to teach her the rudimentary skills to control her magic. She thought he was the best person for the job, but she worried that he'd be angry when he met the woman who had bitten her and turned her too. Still, Letta thought this might be best for everyone. And what if her brother and she had a sister they didn't know about? Though she didn't want Hannah to let it go to her head if they learned she was a princess too.

When they arrived, Letta wondered what the king might have done with the fae seers. She smiled when her boy-like grandfather spied them in the scorpion fae's woods.

"Back so soon. Not another fae seer—" The king abruptly stopped speaking. "She is the lost one." Then he frowned. "A wolf too?" He tilted his chin up. "The one who bit and turned you."

He was wiser than anyone Letta had ever known.

"Hannah just came into her scorpion fae abilities. I was hoping you might teach her some of the rudiments of controlling her magic, like you did for me when I was younger."

He let out his breath and nodded. "You will have jobs to do also, Hannah."

"I want to go with them to trick-or-treat," Hannah blurted out, as if nothing else was important.

"She never got to go when she was little," Letta explained.

"She has to have some control over her magic before she can go anywhere," the king said sternly. "However, if she works hard and shows me that she can control it, well, we'll see."

"You said she was the lost one. What did you mean by that?" Simon asked.

"Her mother was with a wolf pack and she fell in love with a scorpion fae. No one in their right mind would marry a scorpion fae. We're just too warlike for our own good. But she loved him and he loved her and they were together long enough to have a baby girl. Her pack kicked her out, and we took them in, but during the wars between scorpion fae clans, Hannah's father died, and since Carmel wasn't a scorpion fae and she couldn't return to her pack, she just disappeared. We tried to locate her because the baby was half scorpion fae, but we were so busy fighting our own battles, we lost them for good. Until now, it seems." He gave Hannah a small smile. Then to Letta and Simon, he said, "Leave her with us. We'll take good care of her and you can visit us whenever you have the time."

Hannah looked so disappointed, like the fae magic didn't mean anything to her, only being with them to trick-or-treat did.

Letta gave her a hug. "We'll be back for you. Don't you worry."

"We will," Simon agreed.

"Come, Hannah. The sooner we get started, the sooner we'll have you back with the wolf pack. Don't worry. I'm not keeping you here permanently. As you can see, all the ones I lead here are...underage, but you. I'll make an exception for you. No more foster homes for you." Then he frowned. "Not that I can't handle it, but...you do have your shifting under control, don't you?"

Letta suspected her grandfather worried that Hannah might turn all of his charges into wolves. She smiled and gave her grandfather a hug and kiss. When the kids got older, he would lose the glamor and show them how old he truly was, so they'd mind him. Letta hoped Hannah wouldn't act up and would take orders from what appeared to be a child-king.

Letta took hold of Simon's hand to leave and repeated to Hannah, "We'll be back."

One of the younger fae began to play music to soothe the soul, and Letta smiled. Maybe even Hannah could play music that well one day.

When she and Simon finally returned to the cottage, they heard Mark and Bryan shouting. "No, grab...uh, just, if Simon and Letta see what a mess—"

Letta opened the door and both puppies and Mark and Bryan looked up from the mess the puppies had made with paper, torn and shredded all over the floor. They looked like they'd played tug-of-war with it and the men.

"Sorry," Bryan said. "Uh, are we free to take on some gardening jobs?" He looked hopeful.

Letta smiled. "Yeah, but after you clean up this mess. Didn't you get them a tug-of-war toy?"

"Even our wolf pups have rope chew toys we use to train them in play for when they are adults and can compete in the games," Simon said.

Mark pointed at the pristine rope toy. "I think it's a little big for them yet."

"Hannah stayed with your grandfather?" Bryan asked.

"Yes, he's a master magic user, but he's also very good at teaching all ages how to control their magic." Letta explained about Hannah's parents.

"No one knows what happened to her mother then?"

Mark asked.

"No. The king didn't even know what had become of the baby girl. He'll take good care of her."

"She won't be able to return for Halloween, will she?" Bryan asked.

"Only if she gets her magic under control. She might have to wait until next year."

"But she'll be returning to live with us, won't she?" Bryan asked.

Letta smiled. "Yes. This is her home. My grandfather won't keep her there any longer than he has to, once he's sure she will be safe to be around."

***

Two weeks later, it was the night before Halloween and Simon and Letta had traveled to see her grandfather and check on how Hannah was doing. She was practicing with the younger ones, half her age, and frowned to see Simon and Letta turn up. "I'm not ready." She sounded so disappointed.

King Tameron shook his head. "If by tomorrow night she is doing well enough, I'll take her." His other charges looked hopeful he'd take them too. He smiled. "Of course. You too."

***

The next night, twenty-five of Simon's pack members of all ages wanted to go trick-or-treating, something they'd never done before. Even two of his older council members were going. He couldn't believe it, but he was glad so many wanted to enjoy this. He just wished he could cheer Letta up. She'd been so disappointed the night before when her grandfather had said Hannah wasn't ready to go anywhere. Council member Steel opted to stay home and watch the puppies, now called Hans and Greta.

They met with Ena and Brett at their castle, and except for Muriel, who was staying to watch their puppies, the rest of their staff was dressed for the fun.

They went along with Mark and Bryan's suggestion that they hit some homes in one of the developments near where they used to live where the homeowners gave out tons of candy. Mark and Bryan hadn't figured out how to use glamor to hide their ages, so Letta used her magic to help them out. When she made them appear to be five-year-olds, they frowned at her. She laughed. Five-year-olds with attitude.

Simon was glad to see Letta enjoying herself finally. He had decided to be a pirate and she was a fairy princess, just like she'd said she'd wanted to be. Mark and Bryan were dressed like they normally were as the fae. Some were witches and ghosts and vampires. Everyone was having a great time, just as though they were little kids, eager to fill their sacks with candy.

But then Letta grabbed Simon's hand and smiled. "There. Robin Hood and Maid Marion."

Simon looked in the direction she was watching and saw the king and a younger version of Maid Marion. "He brought her."

"And all the rest of the kids, except for a couple of

older ones. They're probably stuck with fae seer guard duty."

Letta waved at Hannah and the king, and Simon waved to get their attention too. One of the younger kids with the king tugged at his hand and pointed in their direction. He smiled and led them toward Simon, Letta, and their pack members, Ena and Brett and their staff.

Letta and Hannah hugged and Ena smiled and said privately to Simon, "I'm glad she is getting along so well with Letta."

"I think Letta is good for her," Simon said.

"And Letta's good for you, Simon."

"And for you," Simon said. "Can you say you would ever have brought your people here for trick-or-treating without her suggesting it?"

Ena cast him an elusive smile. "No."

Then they saw trouble headed their way. Three male teens who were staring at the huge number of fae. Yes, they had invaded the human world just for treats. No tricking this time. But Simon was sure they were three fae seers. Too many fae for them to handle however. He noticed King Tameron also watching them. And then he waved his hands and the three teens disappeared.

Ena frowned. "I wonder what Robin Hood did with them."

"That's Tameron, king of the scorpion fae."

"Oh, wow. Letta's grandfather, then," Ena said.

Tameron caught their eye, smiled, bowed graciously, and headed to the next house with his charges. They didn't need fae glamor. They were the right age to trick-or-treat.

"Where did he send the fae seers?" Simon asked Letta when she and Hannah rejoined him.

"Back to his home. He'll keep an eye on them when he returns."

Simon wondered just how many fae seers the old scorpion king could manage before he couldn't handle all of them.

"He has powerful magic," Letta said, kissed him, and ran off to the next house with her princess bag already partly full, Hannah racing after her.

He laughed and hurried to catch up to them.

"I imagine his magic is more powerful than mine," Brett said, as he and Ena ran after them. "I couldn't have sent the fae seers back to our world like that." He waved his wand, scattering sparkles of light about. Though he had powerful magic, this was just for showmanship and fun.

"We could show them real magic," Ena said.

"Turning into dragons," Brett said.

"And wolves," Hannah said, laughing.

And they all piled up on the next house's doorstep, shouting, "Trick-or-treat!"

After they had their fun with trick-or-treating as younger kids, they were finding an older kids party to crash. *That* was the fae way.

ABOUT THE AUTHOR

Bestselling and award-winning author **Terry Spear** has written over sixty paranormal romance novels and seven medieval Highland historical romances. Her first werewolf romance, *Heart of the Wolf,* was named a 2008 *Publishers Weekly*'s Best Book of the Year, and her subsequent titles have garnered high praise and hit the *USA Today* bestseller list. A retired officer of the U.S. Army Reserves, Terry lives in Spring, Texas, where she is working on her next werewolf romance, continuing her new series about shapeshifting jaguars, writing Highland medieval romance, and having fun with her young adult novels. When she's not writing, she's photographing everything that catches her eye, making teddy bears, and playing with her Havanese puppies. For more information, please visit www.terryspear.com, or follow her on Twitter, @TerrySpear. She is also on Facebook at http://www.facebook.com/terry.spear. And on Wordpress at:

Terry Spear's Shifters
http://terryspear.wordpress.com/

ALSO BY TERRY SPEAR

Romantic Suspense: Deadly Fortunes, In the Dead of the Night, Relative Danger, Bound by Danger

The Highlanders Series: Winning the Highlander's Heart, The Accidental Highland Hero, Highland Rake, Taming the Wild Highlander, The Highlander, Her Highland Hero, The Viking's Highland Lass

Other historical romances: Lady Caroline & the Egotistical Earl, A Ghost of a Chance at Love

Heart of the Wolf Series: Heart of the Wolf, Destiny of the Wolf, To Tempt the Wolf, Legend of the White Wolf, Seduced by the Wolf, Wolf Fever, Heart of the Highland Wolf, Dreaming of the Wolf, A SEAL in Wolf's Clothing, A Howl for a Highlander, A Highland Werewolf Wedding, A SEAL Wolf Christmas, Silence of the Wolf, Hero of a Highland Wolf, A Highland Wolf Christmas, A SEAL Wolf Hunting; A Silver Wolf Christmas, A SEAL Wolf in Too Deep, Alpha Wolf Need Not Apply, A Billionaire in Wolf's Clothing

SEAL Wolves: To Tempt the Wolf, A SEAL in Wolf's Clothing, A SEAL Wolf Christmas; SEAL Wolf Hunting, SEAL Wolf in Too Deep

Silver Bros Wolves: Destiny of the Wolf, Wolf Fever, Dreaming of the Wolf, Silence of the Wolf; A Silver Wolf Christmas, Alpha Wolf Need Not Apply

Highland Wolves: Heart of the Highland Wolf, A Howl for a Highlander, A Highland Werewolf Wedding, Hero of a Highland Wolf, A Highland Wolf Christmas

Billionaire in Wolf's Clothing

www.ingramcontent.com/pod-product-compliance
Lightning Source LLC
Chambersburg PA
CBHW020346180626
46812CB00001B/361